Time Trap

– RICHARD SMITH –

Time Trap is a fascinating book aimed at 9-12 year-olds, but which, like Harry Potter will attract readers of all ages.

It combines mystery and suspense with a well-researched portrayal of life in London in 1862.

As the story unfolds it thus has educational as well as entertainment value in what is a thoroughly good read.

Sir Peter Heap K.C.M.G.

An environmentally friendly book printed and bound in England by
www.printondemand-worldwide.com

www.fast-print.net/store.php

Time Trap
Copyright © Richard Smith 2012

The author would like to thank George Smith, who supplied the original sketches, which were the
source for the fabulous illustrations and cover design.

Original map design by Richard Smith using numerous historical sources

ISBN 978-178035-385-2

First published 2012 by
FASTPRINT PUBLISHING
Peterborough, England.

To my mum, Sylvie, my greatest inspiration

Who wants to be in a street gang?
Jamie does!
To get Todd's backing and join the Riverside
Posse, he takes him to see a secret laboratory.
But disaster is about to strike...

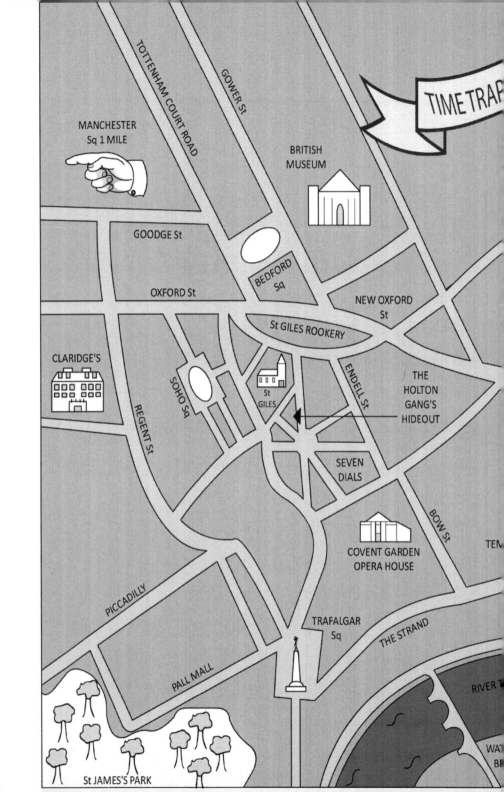

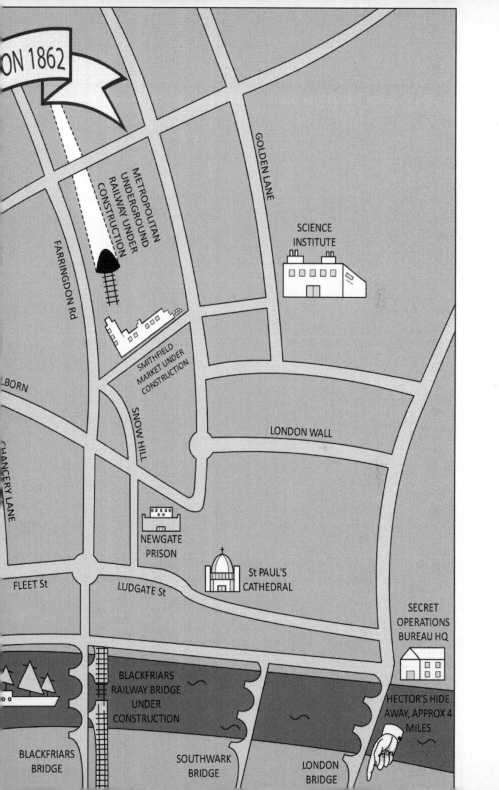

1

Todd's question lingered in Jamie's thoughts as he stood at the window in his Uncle Simon's office, looking out at the huge oval gardens of Bedford Square, enclosed by dark, wrought-iron railings.

The gardens opposite were always locked, much to Jamie's annoyance. He had always longed to explore them when he was much younger, and visited with his parents. Today, he had made the journey from Canterbury to London without them for the first time, having only his school friend, Todd, as company.

Todd sat facing a flat-screen monitor. The rest of the desk on which it stood was filled with neatly stacked books and papers. A row of filing cabinets ran along the wall behind him. Jamie couldn't help but notice that Todd was not in the least bit interested in his Uncle Simon's books or files, or Bedford Square - he just wanted to get into the computer. At least he was keen to see the mysterious engineer's secret laboratory, as promised. And so was Jamie.

'Well, *have* the ghosts been seen since?' Todd asked again.

Jamie clenched his jaw. He wished now that he had never mentioned the old ghost story connected to Simon's house. He'd only brought it up to distract Todd, who'd been bored by their long tube journey - which would have been even longer, if it were not for Todd's good sense of direction. That, thought Jamie, is going to come in handy in London, too.

Todd stood up and checked his gelled, spiky hair in a mirror on the wall. '*Well?* Have they?' he demanded forcibly, fiddling with one of the spikes.

'I don't think so,' Jamie finally replied.

'Ain't much of a story, then,' Todd grumbled.

Simon came into the room, with three plates of sausage-and-mash on a tray. 'Let's go and have lunch in the library upstairs,' he said. 'There's more room in there, and you can see where you'll be doing your projects.'

'Yeah, OK,' Jamie replied.

He followed his uncle into a spacious hallway. Its walls were covered with black-and-white photos, taken in Victorian times, showing London landmarks.

Opposite the stairs hung a wall-clock which Jamie remembered from when he was a kid, with a pendulum that swung as it ticked.

'I forgot to ask, how's your astronomy coming along?' Simon asked, leading the way up the stairs.

'Good! Dad bought me a great telescope last month.'

'Yes, he told me. And you're going to Hawaii soon, I hear. Something about visiting a telescope atop a volcano? You must be very excited about that.'

Jamie heard Todd sigh behind him, as he replied, 'You bet! We're going next weekend, I can't wait! It's a dormant volcano, mind, Mount Mauna Kea. I think they're going to let me operate a telescope that's up there.'

'Excellent! Be sure you send me a postcard.'

Simon pushed open the door to a sun-filled room and laid the tray on a large wooden table.

'Hawaii,' Todd whispered contemptuously, still standing behind Jamie.

'I'll get the drinks,' said Simon and left the room.

Jamie's hands were angrily clenched fists when he turned to Todd. 'You know I'm going there to see their great telescopes.'

'Yeah, right, and I'm going to Broadstairs this year. You're just a snob.'

'I'm not a snob!' Jamie said, bristling.

Their eyes locked in a staring match. 'Don't start dissing me,' Todd warned. Jamie hated the slang words Todd used; 'dissing' was one of them. 'I'll mash you up like I did Ian last week.'

Jamie had been present when the fight took place at the school's main entrance. Todd had been in three fights over the last term; winning all of them had given him quite a reputation. Jamie didn't want to end up like Ian, so he relented. 'OK, OK, I'm a snob.' Ignoring Todd's threatening scowl, he sat down at the table. Todd was just jealous.

Simon soon returned with another tray of drinks and biscuits. 'So, Todd, are you older or younger than my nephew?'

'We're both 13,' replied Todd, 'but I'm two months older.'

'I see,' nodded Simon. Placing the tray down, he asked, 'And how did you chip that front tooth of yours?'

'Football. Last year. In an away match with Winthrop High. I fell against the post.'

Jamie sniggered. 'I heard about that game. You tripped over your bootlaces!'

'I'm good though,' Todd insisted. 'They call me 'the midfield general'.'

'And what about you, Jamie? Made the team yet?'

'That won't happen unless someone chops off one of his two left feet!' joked Todd.

Jamie shook his head. 'No, but the teacher said I'm getting better.'

'Glad to hear it. So how's everyone back home?'

'Fine. Dad still keeps promising to take me fishing. And if I remember rightly, you said you were going to take me sea-fishing.'

'You're right, I did say that, but I've been awfully busy. I'm lucky I could manage to get this weekend with you in. Can I make it up to you with a kick-about in the park tomorrow morning?'

Jamie smiled. 'I suppose so.'

'Splendid. We're going to go to the engineer's lab at the British Museum later, it's practically around the corner.'

'Can't wait for that,' said Todd, then looked at Jamie. 'Ask him about the ghosts,' he mouthed.

Jamie gave a stern shake of the head and mouthed back, 'No!'

***

When Todd had finished his meal, he reached over to several stacks of copper and silver coins on the table and picked up a large silver one.

'I got those out so you could take a look,' said Simon. 'I know your projects are about Victorian science, but the coins will give you a feel for those days.'

'What would all this be worth in today's money?' Todd asked, stroking the coin with his thumb.

Simon thought for a moment. 'I'd say about £80.'

'Cool. So what do you know about this engineer?' Todd asked. 'Jamie told me he lived here - I mean, in this house.'

Simon nodded. 'That's right. He came from a wealthy family and back then it was usual for such young men to enter the army. Hector wanted to be an engineer, but his father insisted he joined the army. So they compromised, Hector joined the Royal Engineers when he was 17. He proved to be such a good soldier – though, what I can gather, a bit of a nutcase – that the Queen's Royal Regiment acquired him, and he went on to become a captain. He was involved in a fairly big war, the first Afghan War. He was badly wounded in that one, and left the army soon afterwards. He was 33.'

'So, was he brave?' Todd asked.

'I'd say so! And he took some enormous risks. During a war with Burma, he rescued five men from the jungle, under heavy fire. Five times he ran to get them, one by one, and carry them on his shoulder to safety.'

Todd laughed. 'Cool.'

'He had a truly good friend in the Army. They fought side by side on occasion. He lived not far from here, in Manchester Square. After Hector left the Army, this chap went on to become a colonel. Colonel Ramsbottom was his name.'

Todd sniggered. 'What a name!'

'Maybe a funny name but, like Hector, he was a brave soldier. I have his journal downstairs. It describes various campaigns in which they served together. It's actually the original. It's really interesting. Jamie, would you mind getting it? It's in the back room on a table, in a red folder. Be careful with it, mind.'

Jamie couldn't wait; he'd known about the journal and always wanted to read it. He hurried down the stairs, just as he used to when he was much younger; hopping down two at a time and holding on to the banister. He passed the wall-clock and went into the back room, which was a lot less tidy than the front office. Spotting the big red folder sitting on a mound of books, he picked it up and went to leave the room. It was then that something in the far corner caught his eye. Even before turning, he instinctively knew this was strange. Then he looked and saw them: two grainy, faceless figures...

//

Jamie's heart was pounding as he climbed the stairs in a daze, with tears blurring his vision.

'Jamie, are you OK?' Simon asked, alarmed by his nephew's white face.

'I've just seen the two ghosts,' he whispered, putting the folder down.

Todd laughed. 'Good one, Jamie, but you can't frighten me.'

'I saw them,' Jamie said firmly. 'They were in the back room.' He shivered, and hugged himself. 'I don't believe in ghosts - but I *saw* them. They were really there.'

'This is incredible,' said Simon, shaking his head and ushering Jamie to a chair. '*I've* never seen them.'

'Jamie's already told me a bit about them, but what actually happened?' Todd asked.

Simon frowned and glanced towards Jamie. 'I don't think this is the time, Todd.'

'Jamie don't mind, do you, Jamie?'

Jamie shrugged.

'Very well,' said Simon with a sigh. 'I certainly don't believe the story, and there's not much to it, really. It was around the time Hector was living here. One winter's night, there'd been a tip-off about some house thieves. The area was crawling with police; a couple of them followed two suspects into this house. The story goes that the coppers had them cornered, and then they disappeared before their very eyes. If you ask me, the police who were chasing the thieves lost them, and made up the story to save face.' He hesitated. 'Jamie, what you saw could have been a trick of the light. These things do –'

'No, Simon, it wasn't. I know what I saw.'

Simon seemed perplexed. 'What you need is a strong cup of tea,' was all he said.

Jamie shook his head, but Simon was adamant.

Todd studied Jamie, smirking. 'What are you playing at, Jamie? We've not even been here an hour yet and you've seen the ghosts already. So what did they look like?'

Jamie recollected. 'Just, dark shady figures, looking right at me!' he said.

Todd's smirk remained. 'But who was they? What about their faces?'

'They didn't have faces.'

Todd went to the open window and looked out. 'They'll be having a match now, back home,' he said. 'Turbo polishing his skills; Fatty Freddy in goal. He's useless! Don't know how he got to be our second keeper. Good job Javheed never got injured or we'd never have finished third, even. I'd text Jonesy and tell him he'll never be as good as me, if my mum hadn't taken my phone.' Todd squawked, imitating his mother: '"You can't go to London with your mobile, you're only 13, it'll get pinched." I blame *your* mum, it was her idea.' He paused for a moment then pulled out a catapult. 'Someone's left a shopping bag across the street. Wonder if I can pick it off.' He searched his pockets. 'Damn, no stones left.'

'You wouldn't have hit it at this distance with the small stones you had,' Jamie told him. 'Too light. Not accurate enough.'

Todd moved away from the window, frowning at Jamie. 'What the hell do you know about catapults?' He crossed the room to a door in the corner, and opened it. Then he gasped and jumped back in fear. 'Oh my God, it's the ghosts!'

Jamie bolted upright from his chair, which crashed to the floor behind him.

Todd grinned broadly. 'Gotcha!' he cried, triumphantly.

'That's not funny, Todd! You knob!'

'Knob, eh?' Laughing, Todd jumped on Jamie, and got him in headlock. 'Who's the knob now, eh?' He ruffled Jamie's hair with his knuckles.

'I've told you, Todd - *don't do that!* It hurts!'

'I'm surprised you haven't learned to stop dissing me by now.'

'Stop! I can't breathe,' Jamie squawked.

Todd released his grip. 'You do not call a member of the Riverside Posse a knob without getting punished. You're not in the gang, yet.' Assuming a boxing stance, he challenged Jamie: 'Ready to take me on?'

'You've only been boxing five times and you think you can beat the world,' Jamie scoffed, smoothing his hair with the flat of his hand.

'I can beat *you*. Anyway, I think we should go on a ghost-hunt, tonight, what do you say?'

Jamie rubbed his neck and picked up the chair. He was beginning to wish he'd never let Todd come. Here he was, having seen two ghosts, and Todd was roughing him up.

Todd brought out his catapult again. 'Why did you bring *that,* anyway?' asked Jamie. 'You're useless with it!.'

'Because I like it and I need the practice. Have you heard about the battles we've had with that gang at the old factory?' he asked with a grin. Jamie nodded. 'It's well mental! Because they've got air-guns, they keep getting the better of us. Javheed's cousin said he can get hold of some air-guns. We'd give them a good battle then.'

Todd took some of the Victorian coins from the table and stuffed them into his pocket. 'Whoa, these weigh a ton! Hey, they might be worth something to a collector.'

'Put them back, Todd,' said Jamie.

Simon came in with the tea. 'Here we are. How are you feeling, Jamie?'

'Not bad,' Jamie replied, but it wasn't exactly true; apart from Todd's antics stealing the coins and bullying, the ghostly experience was still fresh.

'Tell us more about the engineer, Simon,' Todd urged.

Simon glanced at Jamie. 'OK with you, if I carry on?'

Jamie nodded and picked up a pen, ready with his notepad, thinking that if he could start on his project, it would take his mind off the ghosts.

'Some years after leaving the army, Hector joined an exploratory expedition to China in 1852. He turned up in Shanghai four years later like a man possessed, demanding a ship take him home.'

'Why? What *happened* to him in China?' Todd asked, leaning forward.

Simon shrugged. 'But we do know he started working with the Government when he got back to England. On what, nobody knows. It was top secret. And it still is! He disappeared not long afterward, in 1861, never to be seen again.'

'What happened?' Todd asked.

'I'd say something scared him. His assistant, Catherine Wallace, knew something. Jamie's fascination with astronomy began because I used to tell him about her, when he was little - didn't it, Jamie? She was a good astronomer and studied at the Science Institute.'

'Where was the Science Institute?' Jamie asked, pen at the ready.

'Golden Lane, Barbican. She was one of the last people to see Hector, and I reckon she knew something.'

***

'Are you going to put those coins back?' Jamie asked Todd, when Simon left the room to get ready for the museum.

'Give it a rest, Jamie. When you join the Posse, *you* might have to nick something.'

Jamie pondered on being in the Posse. He would be recruited to fight the gang with the air-guns for sure, but he would be on a par with Todd and the others, which meant no more bullying from Wayne Carter. And he'd soon be able to hide out with them at the river in the old, disused boating shed.

It was the reason Jamie organised this trip: Todd would get to see London and the engineer's lab, and he, Jamie, would get to join the gang.

Jamie's gaze fell on the red folder containing the Colonel's journal. Taking a black book from the folder, he gently fanned the brittle, yellowish pages and began to read the Old English writing.

5th February 1839

We've been moved to Hyderabad near the Afghan border as things are hotting up. As I've written before in my journal, I have little time for politics, but it's hard not to avoid the mounting political scrum. Afghanistan needs help to prevent a Russian invasion which would threaten the security of British India. The British Government wants to put Shah Shuja back in power, replacing Dost Mohamed, but three questions arise: How would the fiercely independent Afghan tribesmen react to British aggression? To the restoration of a former ruler of dubious popularity? And how, even if we succeed, could the British hold on to Afghanistan?

Jamie moved on a few pages.

10th March 1839

The invasion of Afghanistan begins. Under the command of Lieutenant-General John Keane, we head for Kandahar through the Bolan Pass, a huge chasm, running between preciptitous rocks for 70 miles. The invasion force stretches for miles, a vast, unwieldy column of soldiers, beasts and wagons.

25th April 1839

Took Kandahar without much fuss. Shuja enters the city in apparent triumph. I find the inhabitants somewhat rude and charmless. The city is beastly dirty. We stay for two miserable months, waiting for the harvest to ripen.

Simon came back into the room. 'How's it going?'

'I'm reading the Colonel's journal.'

'Oh, yes, you'll enjoy that.' Simon said. 'We'll go and see Hector's lab in about five minutes, OK?'

A bright flash of lightning reflected off the walls, followed by a distant rumble of thunder. Simon hurried to shut the window. Looking up at the sky, he said, 'My, goodness, it's gone dark out there. I'd better go and shut the windows downstairs.'

When Simon had gone, Todd demanded the journal.

'Yeah, OK, in a minute.' Jamie carefully turned some more of the ancient pages and read further.

29th June 1839

The fortress town of Ghazni stands in our path and Keane wants to take it. Spies inform us that it's almost abandoned and the defences are weak.

21st July 1839

The spies' reports have no doubt come from, and been instructed by, the enemy. What confronts us is an impressive fortress. Hector is itching to enter it. He has that burning desire for war in his eyes. He suggests to Keane that the engineers are put to work to find a chink in the barricades. Keane agrees.

22nd July 1839

At midnight, three engineers and a party of Indian sappers stack 300 pounds of gunpowder at the Kabul Gate. A magnificent explosion follows, louder than thunder. Before we storm the breach, Hector recites his usual remark, about having a drink in the Guards' Club. He and I fight side by side, scything through the warriors. Hector fights like a demon, first discharging his six pistols, then going to work with his rifle, giving one Ghazi the butt and another the cold steel of his bayonet. Entering the city takes some time -

Jamie peered up from the book. Wait a minute. What if Hector and Ramsbottom were both killed and the two ghosts were them? No, Hector disappeared in 1861 and the diary was dated 1839. Jamie resumed.

Entering the city took some time but by sun-up the citadel is in British hands and I acquire an ornamental spear. We lose a lot of men, some of them officers.

As the distant thunder grew louder, it seemed to Jamie that the guns he was reading about were coming to life.

20th August 1839

The order has been given for British troops to withdraw back to India. Now the Russians recognise that Afghanistan will remain a British sphere of influence. Hector and I stay with the garrison at Kabul, our drink in the Guards' Club will have to wait.

Jamie flicked forward a few more pages.

2nd November 1841

The insurrection explodes in Kabul with an attack on the British Residency. The large courtyarded mansion comes under siege. Everyone inside is killed by the mob. Things are hotting up again.

24th November 1841

Rebels open fire on us from a hilltop with long-range rifles. Hector gathers some men and they use the lone artillery gun to good effect, but eventually it overheats, allowing the Afghans to close to within a few yards. I help to defend the gun as intense fighting ensues, but we are overpowered and lose it.

Jamie, Todd,' called Simon from downstairs. 'Let's go, before it really starts to pour down.'

As Todd snatched the journal from Jamie and placed it on the table with a triumphant laugh, another flash of lightning reflected off the walls, quickly followed by thunder.

When they left the house for the British Museum, Todd pulled up the hood on his top, covering his baseball cap. Jamie, like Simon, was wearing a coat; he pulled it around him more tightly as the storm grew in force. Moments later, they were blasted by torrential rain as a succession of lightning flashes lit up the gloom.

Todd hurried ahead. He spun round to face Jamie and Simon, and said, 'It's like the *paparazzi* are taking shots of us!'

It seemed that every three or four seconds thunder crashed overhead.

Jamie liked thunderstorms, but he'd never experienced such a storm as the one raging above him now. The high surrounding buildings will take a strike rather than it hitting us, he thought, but he knew they could still be injured if a tree was hit and fell. 'We should hurry,' he told the others.

'OK, let's run,' agreed Simon.

They were drenched by the time they raced through the gates. Catching sight of the row of large, white pillars supporting the building, Jamie remarked, 'This looks like something out of ancient Rome.'

'Come on,' urged Simon. 'We need to get inside.' Yet another heavy burst of thunder filled the air as a dazzling fork of lightning flashed above the museum, highlighting it against the dark clouds.

'That's proper mental!' cried Todd in awe.

'Yeah - but I love it!' said Jamie.

At the top of the steps, a man in uniform held the door open for them. Simon greeted him as he shrugged off his coat. 'Give me yours, boys,' he said, 'and I'll put them in the cloakroom.' As they waited for him, a succession of lightning flashes lit up the foyer, followed almost instantly by more loud claps of thunder, each of which shook the building.

Moments later, they followed Simon down some concrete steps behind the cloakroom, away from the ferocious storm.

The further they descended into the gloom below, lit only by dull light bulbs dangling from cables, the colder it became. Jamie brushed his hand across the bare-bricked wall as they passed along a narrow corridor with doors on either side. Even down here, he could hear the violent storm.

Simon stepped through an open doorway into a small office, and came out with a bunch of keys in his hand. Then he crossed the room to the far wall and unlocked an older, wooden door.

Jamie heard Todd gasp when the lights were switched on, revealing countless test-tubes, bottles and jars set up on a wooden bench for an experiment. At the centre of the apparatus sat a large, four-necked bottle with rubber tubes connected to it, apparently linking all the equipment together.

'Wow!' Todd whispered. 'This is like being those archaeologists who discover a pharaoh's tomb.'

Simon laughed. 'That's exactly what we thought when we found it.'

'When *was* that?' Jamie asked, looking at the bookshelves that lined every wall.

'Early last year. The entrance had been bricked up and decorated over. Some scientific papers that were found recorded that work had been carried out under the museum, so we went in search of a laboratory. Hector started his work in this room in 1856, and whatever he was working on would be the first and last experiment to take place here.'

Jamie looked up from scribbling in his notebook. 'What was the lab like when you first saw it?'

Simon grunted. 'Full of cobwebs and dust. But, otherwise, this is exactly how it looked when we found it.'

Todd walked slowly around the bench to a huge fireplace and stared up at the large painting of a stern-faced man with a telescope by his side, hanging above it. 'Who's this then?'

'Sir Isaac Newton,' Simon told him. 'A great scientist and the man who discovered gravity. He always looks to me as if he is guarding the lab.'

Todd turned back to the bench. 'I bet it was great in here with stuff all bubbling away inside these tubes and bottles and all that.' Then, spotting something strange at the far end of the room, he asked, 'What's *that?*'

Jamie followed him over to a big iron arch on a plinth, which reached almost to the ceiling. They stared at each other, and then at the object in front of them.

'Yes - what is this, Simon?' said Jamie, frowning deeply.

Simon shook his head. 'That's something else we don't know. Hector's scientific papers have never been found, but we know he began working on this for the Government after returning from China.' He patted the arch. 'It's a another mystery he took to his grave.'

Todd stared at the electric cables that sprouted through holes in the wall next to the arch. 'So what are the wires for?'

'We're having alarms installed at last. Those cables go upstairs to a control panel. The engineers will be back tomorrow to complete the job. Which reminds me, I must dig out their invoice. Sorry, boys, but you'll both have to come with me while I go next door. Won't take long.'

In the adjoining office, Jamie stood with Todd in the doorway, watching Simon rummage through a filing cabinet.

Todd screwed up his face. 'I was enjoying looking around in there.' He watched the historian with suspicion. 'He's going to be ages, his sort always are.' He tilted his head. 'Come on.'

'We can't. Simon won't like it.'

'He'll be all right. We'll say we was overcome with history and science and had to go back in there.'

'This is real cool,' Todd said, as they stepped back into the laboratory. With the storm still raging overhead, he moved towards the bench. Jamie joined him just as a loud crash of thunder rattled the glassware on the bench, and made him jump.

'Wicked!' cried Todd, eyeing the huge arch. Within a moment, he was stroking its dull, solid surface.

'What do you reckon it was?' Jamie asked, touching the strange structure more tentatively.

Todd shrugged. 'Don't ask me, but it's... sort of interesting.'

Suddenly, a devastating explosion rocked the lab, and a massive charge arced from the alarm cables to the arch, filling the lab with a blinding white light. Jamie lurched against Todd; then they both fell, and lay cowering on the stone floor.

III

A few seconds passed, but it seemed much longer, before the blinding light vanished. Jamie lay on the ground, dazed and in pain. He held his stomach, looking up at the small, blue, electric arcs buzzing between the iron arch.

Todd groaned, rubbing his shoulder and chest. He looked at Jamie. 'Jamie, your nose is bleeding,' he said.

Jamie put his hand to his face, feeling the blood above his mouth. 'What's happened?' He winced. 'Ahh, I've got a bad headache.'

Todd gingerly got to his feet. 'That was some lightning strike. I bet it's done some damage upstairs, because I ache all over.'

'Me too.'

'My head's spinning.' Todd clasped his forehead.

Jamie slowly stood up. 'Simon must have heard that,' he said.

Todd held his ribs. 'He's probably too busy to notice.'

'Well, let's go and tell him.' Jamie made for the next office, but at the door he stopped and frowned. Two men stood there, deep in conversation.

'What's wrong?' Todd asked, sidling next to him.

Jamie shrugged, baffled by the strange uniform one of the men wore; his bushy sideburns and thick moustache looked weird, too! The other man, shorter and stockier, was also a mystery; a thick, wiry, reddish-brown beard contrasted with his bald head. Jamie wiped the last of the blood away, thinking they looked like they'd come from a film set or something.

'Who's that?' Todd whispered.

'They must be in costume, you know, like a theme.'

Todd shook his head. 'They look strange to me,' he said in a whisper.

Jamie hesitated. What had happened to Simon? He entered the room, and asked, 'Where's Uncle Simon?'

Both men spun round. Their stunned expressions soon changed to rage. 'Where have you come from?' the stocky man demanded.

Jamie laughed, uncertain. Pointing a thumb over his shoulder, he replied, 'In there.'

The stocky man grabbed him. 'Who are you? Tell me!'

Fingers dug into Jamie's arm, hurting him, but it was the man's angry red face that scared him the most. Acting on instinct, he yanked his arm free and ran, aware of Todd right behind him. Having dodged past the men, Jamie and Todd sprinted along the corridor, ignoring the calls for them to stop.

Jamie knew something was wrong; *where was Simon?*

They burst into the foyer, stopping only at the museum's open doors, where an icy breeze rushed in. Jamie shuddered; his T-shirt gave little protection.

Dry, crispy leaves swept across the grounds in the freezing wind and slate-grey clouds rolled close overhead, adding gloom to a cold, miserable day.

All was quiet except for a two-horse carriage moving at a gentle trot beyond the main entrance, just visible in a fog that drifted in the breeze. Jamie coughed, breathing in a strong, burning smell which he thought was sulphur, remembered from one of the science lessons. It clung to the back of his throat. He turned to Todd, who was flicking his chipped tooth with his tongue - something he always did when he was scared or excited. 'What's going on? Is this a dream?'

Todd's voice shook. 'If it is, I'm in it.'

The sound of pounding footsteps had Todd looking over his shoulder quickly. 'They're after us. Run!'

They raced from the grounds, over cobbled streets.

Reaching New Oxford Street, Jamie almost forgot how cold he was. Busy horse-drawn traffic rumbled past on the cobbled roadway, the wheels of the carriages creating a continuous roar. The clacking and clattering accompanied the clip-clopping chorus of the horses' hooves. Jamie's mind swirled as he stared at the handcarts pushed by determined-looking men mingling with the traffic. They were carrying everything from baskets of fruit and vegetables to sacks of coal. He detected a familiar smell: manure. He couldn't make up his mind which was worse: the smell of the horse droppings on the road, or the car exhaust fumes he was used to at home. The pavements were packed with pedestrians, from gentlemen in top hats and greatcoats, to women wearing long coats and thick, woollen shawls. Everyone was dressed for the biting cold.

Clouds of frozen breath billowed from Jamie's mouth and his body shook with the cold but, despite his discomfort, he continued to stare at the spectacle before him.

His attention was drawn to a chirpy lad, about the same age as himself, selling newspapers. He wore grimy, threadbare clothing and a shapeless hat, and had to shout to make himself heard over the din of traffic. His voice rang out over and over again: '*The Times*, buy it here! *The Times*: Civil War rages on in America. Read all about it!' As he shouted, he waved a newspaper above his head.

Jamie noticed Todd had been getting odd stares from passers-by. He tried telling him that his spiky hair looked out of place here, but all that came from his mouth was frozen breath.

Todd fumbled for the money he had taken from Simon, and dropped some. Jamie watched nervously as he retrieved the coins and walked over to the paper-seller, whose ink-stained fingers fished out the right money. 'Fanks, chum,' the boy said, and then stared curiously at Todd's hair before resuming his monotonous call.

Todd read the date on the newspaper. 'It's December... 1862!' he whispered. 'No wonder it's freezing, it's Decem... '

'*What!* Did you say *1862?*' said Jamie. 'Battle at Fredericksburg,' he read aloud over Todd's shoulder.

Suddenly, they were grabbed roughly. 'Are these the intruders, gentlemen?' enquired a fat policeman, through his handlebar moustache.

Jamie gaped up at the lawman, confounded by his heavy, dark-blue cape. A tall, black, leather hat sat on his greying head and his stomach swelled in front of him.

'That's them!' bellowed the stocky bald man from the museum.

The policeman checked both ends of New Oxford Street. 'There's a patrol due any minute now. I'll get them taken to Scotland Yard,' he announced.

'No!' The stocky man shook his head. He leaned close to the boys, making a detailed inspection of them and paying particular attention to Todd's spiky hair. 'No, we'll take them back to the museum.'

Todd threw Jamie a worried glance, then said to the policeman, 'Please, we haven't done anything wrong.'

The officer snorted. 'Oh, no?'

'Leg it!' yelled Todd, grabbing Jamie's T-shirt. He ran blindly onto the road, straight into the path of an omnibus. The driver was quick to react, pulling hard on the reins, so that the two horses pulling the vehicle reared up, their front hooves pawing the air. Jamie thought he and Todd were going to be hit by a wagon coming the other way, but they just made it to the opposite kerb as the fat policeman blew hard on his whistle.

Todd led the way, running. 'This way, quick!' The sound of the whistle shrilled in the distance; they had a head-start on the policeman.

They passed a row of shops on a curved road. At the end of the shops, Todd dived into an alley, dragging Jamie with him.

Jamie began to shake uncontrollably. 'What are we going to do? *Do something!*' he sobbed.

'Shut it, Jamie,' Todd hissed, grabbing him by the arms. 'You're in shock. Me too, probably.'

Jamie wiped tears from his cheeks. 'What's happened to us?'

'I haven't got a clue -' Todd stopped mid-sentence. Someone was approaching the alley.

Jamie braced himself. Running footsteps echoed in the street and an urgent voice announced, 'I was just around the corner from Denmark Street when I heard your whistle. What's happened?'

'Two lads,' replied the policeman, standing outside the alley. 'Trying to burgle the British Museum.'

Jamie had heard enough; he crept quietly with Todd to the end of the alley and into a straw and sawdust-strewn courtyard. Jamie peered up at crooked tenement buildings made of timber which was now decaying. The buildings teetered above them, he was amazed that they hadn't collapsed.

Nearby, two freshly slaughtered pigs swung from hooks, blood dripping from their slashed throats and soaking into the straw and sawdust. Some rats had gathered and were drinking the blood. A vile smell hung in the air.

Jamie felt his chest tighten and his breath catch in panic. The stink reminded him of the smell of a dead dog he had once come across in a field. Moments later, he jumped at the sound of a slap and a man's cry from inside a shed on the far side of the yard. The scream was met with a barrage of broad Irish voices. 'Where is he?' a rough voice demanded.

'I'm getting out of here,' Jamie whispered, and made for the alley.

'What about that copper?'

Jamie didn't answer. The sound of the shed doors opening left them little option but to hurry away.

With Jamie setting the pace, they scurried from the alley without a backwards glance, hoping there was no sign of the policemen. Across the road, the tall white spire of a church showed through the fog. The boys ran towards it, through a gate, then sprinted along a gravel path, kicking up stones as they went. Before them stood two big wooden doors, which creaked when they pushed them.

They found themselves in a wood-panelled vestibule and paused, gasping for breath.

Todd swallowed. 'What the hell's happened? And was what all that about, back there?'

Jamie took deep breaths, not yet able to reply.

Todd approached the door to the nave. Inside the church, the vicar was arranging a selection of chalices on a table at the altar. Jamie followed Todd down the red-carpeted aisle.

'Excuse us, Father,' Todd said in a small voice.

The vicar turned, exhibiting a black beard. 'Yes?' he asked, observing their shivering bodies.

Todd backed away, as if nervous of the vicar's black cassock.

The vicar frowned. 'You've been running, haven't you? Why, it's 8.30 in the morning. From whom are you running away?'

'We strayed into an alley, across the road,' said Todd.

'Oh,' said the bearded clergyman. 'You've visited the Rookeries. You must never go there again, it's far too dangerous.' He frowned, studying their T-shirts and jeans and taking a closer look at Todd's hair. 'What have you done to your hair?'

Todd remained speechless, so Jamie stepped in. 'He... spilt some oil on his head, didn't you, Todd?'

Todd nodded.

'And where are your coats?'

Jamie answered again. 'We're lost; we were with my uncle on our way to visit my grandmother but got separated. Our coats are with him.'

'Hmm,' said the vicar narrowing his eyes. 'So why were you running?'

'We're scared, mister,' said Todd desperately. 'Please can we stay here for a while?'

The vicar studied them once more. 'I don't normally take in strays; if it gets around that I'm taking in strays, I'll be inundated. It happened to Father Adams, over at St Martin's, but you can stay... only for a while, though, yes?'

'Yes sir,' Jamie said.

'Very well. Come along. I'll take you to see Lily; I'm sure she can find you each a coat.'

***

Later that day − at three o'clock, according to the church clock's chimes − the boys were sitting in the undercroft below the church. Its white-painted walls and arched ceiling were bathed in candlelight, and an iron stove burned warmly nearby.

For the first time since they'd entered the church, they were alone. Todd's sullen face didn't help Jamie feel any better. He watched Todd pulling the elastic of his catapult. He was now sporting straight hair, having washed away the gel.

Jamie had been tearful all day and had hardly spoken. The past seven hours or so had been a horrible blur. He couldn't stop thinking of his family, or wondering would he ever see them again. Once again, panic clutched at his chest and caught at his breath.

'So what *has* happened to us?' Todd asked, breaking the silence. Jamie looked at him through swollen eyes; a slight shake of the head was the only response he could give. 'How are we going to survive in *this* time?' Todd continued. 'We've got nowhere to stay and no one to help us.'

'Todd, I'm really scared. We're never going to see our families again, have you realised that?' Jamie's eyes began welling with tears again. 'We're going to become missing persons in *our* time and no one will ever know what happened to us. God knows what Simon's going to say, and we were in his care.'

Todd stared at the stone floor. At last he said, 'We have to leave soon, remember?'

Jamie blew his nose. 'I don't think I can take much more of this. I want to go home to my family. *What are we doing in this time? We don't belong here!*'

Todd didn't answer; his stare at the ground was hard and troubled. After a while, he brought out all the coins he'd taken from Simon's library and divided them into two piles. He handed Jamie his share. 'Here, in case we get split up. The money's the only plus in all this. You did get rid of your coins from *our* time, didn't you?'

Jamie nodded, staring at the silver and copper coins, all with the head of Queen Victoria on them. He studied one silver coin and said, 'There's one here called a shilling. I don't know anything about this money.' He gazed down at his trainers. 'What about our clothes? D'you think we look out of place?'

Todd frowned. 'I don't think so. We're both wearing black jeans and T-shirts, nothing odd about that.' He looked down at his footwear. 'My black boots look just like... black boots.' Gazing at Jamie's white trainers he added, 'Your trainers look different, I suppose, but who would know they're not new out? Lily and that vicar didn't say anything, did they?' He pulled a face. 'They talk a bit, sort of... funny, don't they?'

Jamie shrugged. 'I guess – but it's 1862, according to that paper. People won't talk like they do in our time, will they? We must sound strange to them, as well.'

'I s'pose so,' agreed Todd. 'Talking of that newspaper, what's the war going on in America?'

Jamie recalled the headline and the paper-seller's chant. 'I think it's The American Civil War,' he said. 'Can you believe that we're living in the time of it?' He shook his head in amazement.

Todd studied the copper and silver coins in his hands. 'If we ever get split up, we'll meet up here, yeah?'

Jamie didn't reply; his head was still spinning at their predicament.

Todd scratched his head. 'I still think we should go back to the museum and see - '

'No!' Jamie cried. 'We can't go back there; they're after us.'

'But like I said, they might've thought we was trying to nick something. They might know where Hector is.'

'D'you know something, I don't think I can face leaving here. What's out there? What was happening across the road with those Irish guys? They were beating someone up.'

'I don't know, but you better get ready to leave, because the vicar said we've got to.'

Jamie stared at Todd; he could feel his face twisted with anxiety. *'What are we going to do?'* He jumped up; the heat from the stove was stirring his blood and sending a burning sensation through his body. 'I want to go home, I'm scared! Think of something, but not the museum, those men were really evil, God knows what they'd do to us.' He stopped by the brick wall. 'And I don't like what the vicar said about the grounds filled with hundreds of plague victims.' He pointed over his shoulder. 'There could be skeletons behind here.' The vicar had told them many people had died of the Great Plague of London during the mid-17th Century. Jamie imagined zombies smashing through the wall, and stepped away. When he felt at a safe distance he said, 'I've been thinking about those ghosts I saw. I think they were trying to warn me about what was going to happen.'

Todd wasn't listening; he was probing his chipped tooth with his tongue.

'What is it?' Jamie hoped desperately that Todd had come up with something.

'When Simon was telling us about Hector, he said something about his friend in the army? He said they served together.'

'That's right.' Jamie paced the undercroft, keeping clear of the walls. He clicked his fingers trying to recall. 'He said he was a colonel, I read his journal, didn't I? Colonel... Ramsbottom. That's it! Colonel Ramsbottom.'

'That's him. And Simon said he lived in Manchester Square, I remember that because I'm a United fan. *He* must know where Hector is hiding out.'

Jamie breathed heavily; if they wanted to meet the Colonel they would have to venture outside. He felt Todd's eyes on him. He snapped into action, snatching his new coat.

The vicar noticed them as they hurried along the nave. 'Are you leaving now?'

Jamie smiled faintly. 'Yes, and thanks again for the coats.'

'You're welcome. If you don't find your uncle today, try the soup kitchen in Covent Garden.'

'The what?' Todd asked.

'The soup kitchen - it's a place for the needy. They'll give you some food and a bed for the night. It's in Covent Garden.'

Jamie and Todd left the church, only to come to a stop outside the gates in the midst of thickening fog. The surrounding buildings were like big dark shapes, shrouded in the drifting mists, and the gas street lamps were already lit, shining a greenish white light.

'I'm really scared,' said Jamie, looking wearily about. The sooty fog burned his nostrils and the back of his throat. He noticed Todd's silence and could sense that he was scared, too. Gone was his bravado.

Avoiding the alley where they had seen the slaughtered pigs, they set off in search of a cab.

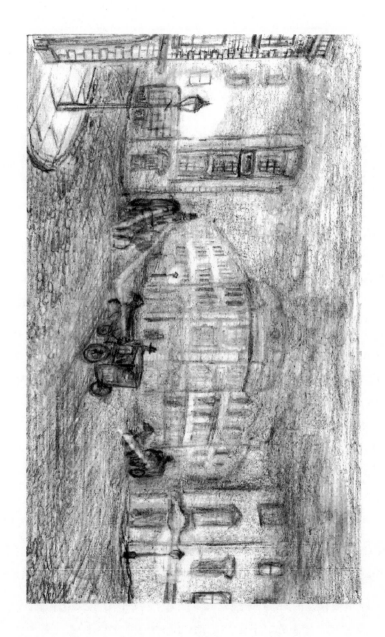

41

IV

The search for a cab proved fruitless. Jamie and Todd were standing on a street corner with dusk beginning to fall.

Jamie watched a flame that seemed to dance inside a street lamp. It burned and flickered, emitting a greenish-white light. He noticed the glass enclosing it was covered in a splattering of coal dust from chimney smoke that swept through the city. What was all this soot doing to people's lungs? What was it doing to *his* lungs?

He began to walk. 'Let's try up here.' He stopped suddenly and whispered, 'Did you hear that?'

'What?' Todd asked, gazing all around.

'Footsteps, they were faint but I heard them behind us.' Jamie stared into the blanket of fog. 'I heard footsteps before, but didn't think much of it.'

'Jamie, we're in London, of course there's going to be footsteps, you div.'

Jamie didn't think he was imagining it. He was now convinced they were being followed. He detected a tapping sound. 'What's that?'

A dark figure emerged from the shroud of fog.

Jamie stood rigid until he saw that the figure was a blind man, probing with a stick. The man passed them as if on a set course, unimpeded by the freezing fog.

Todd shook his head and set off, with Jamie trailing close behind.

They were soon walking along a livelier and busier street, which seemed safer after the deserted area they'd just left. Through the fog, Jamie glimpsed small children still out playing, despite the freezing weather. They would appear and then fade into the fog, hopping and skipping along. One group played a game where they rolled head-over-heels. Jamie and Todd moved through a sea of paupers. Faces peered from everywhere; entire families gathered in the street. Outside one house, a goat stood chained to railings and chickens clucked in small cages. Outside another, Jamie stared up at a large woman barely visible, leaning from an upstairs window, tending to freshly laundered clothes. She hung a sheet over a protruding wooden pole to dry, though it was already grimy from the sooty fog. Jamie soon realised there were many poles along the street with washing fastened and likened them to masses of flags.

Four young men, dressed in dark, heavy clothing, lounged outside a house. 'There was blood all over the floor,' announced one, who wore a tatty top hat. His three friends were laughing as he told his story. 'He won't do *that* again.'

This remark was met with a roar of approval.

Suddenly, emerging from the smog like a couple of shining eyes, came two lights. A large carriage, pulled by two big horses and lit by lanterns, moved slowly through the busy street. As the lingering fog swallowed it again, the boys came to a stationary, shiny, black vehicle next to a street lamp, where the driver was standing high up at the back.

'Are you a mini cab?' Todd asked.

The driver wore all black, including leather gloves. 'A what?' he replied curtly.

'Er, I mean a cab.'

'What do you think?'

Todd looked unsure.

'I think he is a cab,' said Jamie.

Todd looked up again and said, 'Can you take us to Manchester Square?'

'If you've got the money to pay.'

'Yeah, I've got the money,' said Todd, bringing out a handful of coins.

The driver waved them in.

Jamie studied the chestnut horse harnessed to the shaft, then stood on an iron step and opened two small doors. Once on board they sat on an immaculate black leather seat. Jamie liked the two brass lanterns fixed either side of the vehicle, and was pleasantly surprised by the comfortable seat. It was much less comfortable after the driver gave his command, and the horse, slipping on the wet and greasy cobbles, quickened into a trot. As cold air rushed in over the doors, Jamie flicked up the collars of his coat, and Todd quickly followed suit.

***

Manchester Square was a 25-minute ride through London's heavy traffic.

Jamie climbed stiffly out of the cab, then rubbed his numb face as Todd sorted through his coins, helped by the driver, to pay the fare. Although it was now dark, with fog impeding visibility, Jamie could see that the place was similar to Bedford Square with trees in the gardens, but here the houses were fewer and much bigger.

Their cab departed, leaving them standing alone in the square.

'Simon never said what number the Colonel lived at, so what do we do now?' Todd asked, hands in his coat pockets.

Jamie scanned the square. The street lamps were evenly placed, illuminating some of the houses, and gas lights burned beyond many curtains, highlighting their predicament of being stuck out in the cold.

The front door of a house nearby opened, drawing Jamie's eyes to it.

Under the porch lights, a chimney sweep accompanied by a young boy came out of the house. They were both black with soot, more so the boy who carried a sack filled with sticks and brushes over his shoulder. Poor kid, thought Jamie, as the sweep gave the boy a rough nudge and told him to get a move on. Together they then disappeared into the night.

Another man, standing at the doorway, in a black suit, noticed Jamie staring. 'Yes?' he inquired in a clipped voice.

Jamie cleared his throat. 'Could you tell us where Colonel Ramsbottom lives, please?'

'Godfrey is unwell,' said the man, examining them briefly. 'What business do you have with him?'

'He's a friend of my uncle, and my uncle's missing.'

The man pointed. 'He lives on the other side of the square, number 22.'

'Thank you, sir,' said Jamie.

Number 22 was a grand house, with two large pillars at the entrance lit by two hanging brass lanterns. Lights were on downstairs and they took this as a sign of life.

Todd knocked on the door.

On hearing footsteps echoing on bare floorboards, they instinctively stepped back.

'We'll stick with the same story, right?' Jamie said, as someone turned the lock.

'Yes?' asked an elderly man in a loud voice, followed by prolonged coughing.

Jamie's eyes were drawn to an array of medals pinned to the man's silk smoking- jacket. His white hair matched his handlebar moustache. 'I'm Hector Lightfoot's nephew and I'm told Colonel Ramsbottom lives here,' Jamie announced.

The man quelled his spate of coughing. 'I'm Ramsbottom,' he told them, in a loud voice. 'What is all this about?'

'I'm looking for Hector Lightfoot; do you know where he is?' Jamie asked.

'Lightfoot? Yes, he's here.'

'That's great. Could we see him, please?'

After another round of coughing, the man pulled the door open and beckoned them inside. Jamie was impressed with the large rooms and the expensive furnishings, and it was good to be in the warmth again. The man showed them to a big room where a fire provided plenty of heat and the strong smell of stale cigar-smoke lingered.

'Sit down, sit down,' said the Colonel, pointing to two leather, high-backed chairs close to the fire. 'Didn't know Lightfoot had a nephew. What's your name?'

'Jamie.'

'Hmm, he never mentioned you.' He made for the door. 'Wait here, I've got a stew cooking.' He left the room mumbling about hiring a servant, followed by another spate of loud coughing.

Jamie took in the plush furnishings until he meet Todd's stare.

'Where's Hector then?' Todd asked.

Jamie shrugged, then noticed something familiar. 'It can't be,' he whispered in wonder. He got up and reached for a black book on an occasional table next to Todd's chair. 'I don't believe it; this is the Colonel's journal; the one I read in *our* time.'

He grinned at Todd; he was about to meet Hector, but first he thought he'd sneak a look at the journal. He gazed briefly at the door before fanning the pages, trying to pick up from where he'd been interrupted in Simon's library. Todd sighed as Jamie began to read.

24th November 1841

We counter-attack and retrieve the gun. I was knocked down by a blow on the head from an Afghan knife, which would have done for me had I not put a few pages of Blackwood's Magazine in my forage cap. I could feel the blood running down my back as I got up, half-stunned. Seeing that a second blow was coming, I met it with the edge of my sword and removed my assailant's hand. He bolted, but another slashed my shoulder with his sword. As my sword met his following strike, he was shot by an officer. I, too, was fired at; the shot hit my sword, breaking it in two, leaving six inches or so on the handle. I see Hector take a bullet in the lower back and go to his side as the men disperse and retreat. I pray Hector will live when we make it back to the cantonment.

'This is unbelievable; Hector and Ramsbottom fighting hand-to-hand with the Afghans. For their lives!'

Todd shook his head, sighing again.

Jamie read on.

11th December 1841

Hector is making good progress and will be able to walk again, thank God. My injuries get better with each passing day. Hector and I, along with some other officers and women and children are to be held as hostages, for assurance that the British force leave and return to India.

Jamie glanced at the door again before flicking through the pages. The concept of reading the original journal now had Jamie's mind reeling.

7th November 1842

Rescued at last! Major-General Sir William Nott's "Army of Retribution," having recaptured Ghazni and Kabul, liberates us. We're going home!

15th May 1843

Had drinks with Hector and some other officers at the Guards' Club back in dear old London, and an enjoyable time it was, too. But the sad news that Hector is leaving the army for Cambridge to become an engineer leaves a bad taste, though we will still continue to meet up for drinks. As I sit here in my comfortable study, I spare a thought for the 4,500 men who set off for India. Despite the promises of protection and gold given to the rebel chiefs, the column was frequently attacked in the freezing snow-covered passes and out of the 4,500, only a single soul made it back to safety. Hector and I both feel a certain amount of guilt that we didn't go with them.

Jamie replaced the book at the sound of footsteps coming along the hall.

The Colonel returned and headed for a drinks trolley. 'That's better; the stew is simmering nicely. Still think I should get a damn servant. Would you like a whisky, Jamie?'

Jamie frowned. 'Er, no thanks.'

'Not a whisky man, eh? What about a gin?'

'No thanks, Colonel.'

The Colonel addressed Todd. 'What about you, want a drink?'

'No thanks,' Todd replied.

'What regiment are you with, Jamie?' the Colonel asked, pouring his drink.

'Umm, I'm not with any regiment,' Jamie replied, throwing a puzzled glance towards Todd.

With a tumbler of whisky in one hand, the old officer dragged a chair to the fireplace with the other.

Jamie fidgeted awkwardly. 'So... where is he?'

'Who?'

'Hector.'

The man began to laugh, which turned into another round of coughing and spluttering. Jamie joined the Colonel in a bout of laughing, but his merriment was somewhat hollow.

'He's in the study,' the Colonel told them.

'Are they from the army?' Todd asked, pointing to the medals.

The man took a sip of his drink. 'Yes, they are,' he said. He tapped one of them. 'This was earned with Hector when we served in Burma.' With an affectionate huff he said, 'We were talking about our military adventures only earlier today. He was a fine soldier, was Hector, and a good captain. He could have made colonel if he'd remained with the army. I first met Hector when he was about 17 and we were soon involved in fighting with Burma. It was shortly after we secured Rangoon. We became surrounded. During an attack, our general was taken hostage. This was about to undermine everything dramatically, but Hector, along with me and eight other soldiers, accepted a mission. We entered their camp undetected at night and rescued the general amidst a ferocious fire-fight. People thought Hector was mad, you know! He usually carried six or seven loaded pistols and would use them to great effect.'

Todd laughed. 'That's cool.'

Jamie glanced at the journal; he'd already read about that. It was mind-boggling, having read the Colonel's journal at Simon's house, and here he was, larger than life.

'I rescued him when he was seriously wounded in Afghanistan.' He shook his head. 'I never enjoyed the army as much after Hector left.'

Jamie had just read about the conclusion of the Afghan War. Besides, he needed to see Hector. 'Colonel, do you think I could see him, now?' he interjected in a low voice.

'Who?'

'My *uncle*. Hector.'

The old man snapped into life with some more coughing. 'Yes, of course. Come, come.'

Jamie and Todd followed the Colonel from the room as he boomed, 'Hector, your nephew is here to see you. Hector!'

The Colonel opened the door to a lit room and greeted Hector. Eager to glimpse the engineer, Jamie stood next to the old man, but the room appeared empty.

The Colonel approached the fireplace and spoke to a painting hanging above. 'Your nephew is here to see you, Hector.'

Bewildered, Jamie stared at a head-and-shoulders portrait of a young, handsome man in uniform, a scar evident on his right cheek.

The boys shuffled backwards. Colonel Ramsbottom smiled at them. 'Say hello to your uncle, Jamie.'

'But... he's not here,' Todd replied, frowning.

The man huffed. 'What are you talking about? There he is.'

Jamie looked to Todd, who nodded towards the door. Together, they shuffled across the room. The last thing they heard, as they walked swiftly along the hall and out of the house, was the Colonel barking at Jamie to show some respect to his uncle.

Jamie shut the front door and they ran, stopping a few yards later. *'That was creepy,'* he said.

Todd sighed deeply. 'I thought Simon said *Hector* was a nut case.'

'Hmm,' Jamie replied, looking over his shoulder. He shivered. 'I really thought we'd found him.'

He stared hard at Todd and said, 'There's only one thing left to do; we'll have to go back to the museum. If we can avoid those guys who tried to grab us, maybe someone else there might tell us where Hector is.'

Todd nodded. 'We'll go in the morning, but for tonight, I think we should go to that soup kitchen the vicar told us about, in Covent Garden.'

Jamie had visions of tramps and strays hanging out at such a place and didn't fancy it. 'What about trying a hotel? We've got the money.'

'No way, it would be too pricey.'

'What about a lodging house? That would be cheaper.'

'There you go again, rich boy, you just can't rough it, can you?

Jamie switched off; he'd heard it all before, but when Todd mentioned the Hawaiian holiday, his heart sank at the thought of missing out on the chance to see the fabulous island. He stared at a gas lamp shining on the other side of the square and stretched his imagination, pretending it was the Hawaiian sun bathing him in warmth. His thoughts were starkly interrupted, returning him to their present reality, when a dark silhouette inside the gardens moved in front of the lamp's rays.

Jamie gasped.

'What's wrong?' whispered Todd.

'Someone's watching us from inside the gardens. Just pretend everything's all right.'

Todd tutted. 'Jamie, it's your wild imagination, again.'

Jamie spoke in a strained whisper. 'I am staring at a figure in the light from that street lamp.'

'It's probably a tree or something .'

'Trees don't uproot and move about.'

Todd peered at where Jamie was looking. 'Can you still see it?'

'Yeah, someone is definitely in the gardens. I don't like this, Todd. First the footsteps and now someone's watching us.'

'So *you* say.' Todd began to walk. 'Come on, let's get that cab to the soup kitchen.'

As they hurried to it, Jamie kept his distance from the railings, glancing at the dark centrepiece frequently. Todd stayed close.

***

The cab dropped them close to Covent Garden, by a noisy public house in an otherwise deserted street. The inn glowed in the fog, between two dark neighbouring buildings. Jamie noticed two women standing outside the establishment, half-hidden in the shadows. His long stare caught the eye of one of them, who greeted him, 'Ello darling, where you off to?'

The two women stepped into the pub's light, revealing their tatty shawls and blemished complexions.

'We're looking for the soup kitchen. It's supposed to be around here,' said Todd.

The woman linked arms with him. 'You ain't gotta go to no soup kitchen,' she said. 'We've got a place just across there, but first, you can buy us a drink.'

Jamie found himself held firmly in the other woman's arms. He was engulfed by the strong smell of alcohol on her breath before being shoved towards the pub's doors and then through them. Someone was playing an accordion, but they could hardly hear it above the revelry.

Pushed through the rowdy pub, Jamie choked on thick tobacco smoke, which hung in the air above the drunken patrons and intertwined with the dusty gas chandeliers. He could see that the place had once been a stylish establishment, but now neglect showed in the torn, red-velvet curtains and spotted mirrors.

Five scruffy men with unsettling glares greeted the two women.

'Who are these two?' asked a sneering, unshaven man.

'We got 'em outside,' answered one of the women.

'They got any money?' asked one with an unkempt beard.

The woman with her arm around Jamie's shoulders replied, 'Of course they 'ave, look 'ow they're dressed.'

'Well, they can buy the drinks, then,' suggested another.

All eyes were on Jamie and Todd. The woman with Todd nudged him. He stared at her red, blotchy face and discoloured teeth. 'What?' he said.

'You 'eard him, get the drinks.'

Todd stepped back but the woman was quick, fishing a hand in his trouser pocket and bringing out a silver coin. 'This'll do,' she said, gleefully, showing the men the money.

Jamie protested when the other woman made a grab for his pockets. The men laughed, watching the tussle.

'Please,' said Jamie. 'We need our money.'

'We need money an' all, dear,' said the woman, laughing harshly for a moment. Then her mood turned sullen. 'Now 'and it over.'

Todd defied his pilferer and stepped back.

Jamie knew they were in trouble when the bearded man stepped towards them, grabbing Todd's arm and growling, 'Give us your money, or we'll beat you, you little weasel.'

V

A smartly dressed man in a brown tweed suit and bowler hat, looking out of place amongst the locals, appeared at Todd's side, his large chest apparent under his jacket. He grabbed Todd's assailant's arm tightly, causing him to let go at once.

'Hey, what you doing?' the bearded man cried.

'Leave these boys alone,' ordered the big man, in a commanding and confident voice.

One of the men in the group licked his lips vigorously. Jamie knew he was about to attack, but was too scared to call out a warning. Suddenly, the thug lunged at the suited man and, equally quickly, received an elbow to the face, which sent him sprawling to the floor. The mystery rescuer twisted the bearded man's arm up behind his back, making him howl. 'Go, go now!' the suited man ordered Jamie and Todd.

They didn't wait around; hastily, they left the pub, squeezing past the on-lookers.

'That was close,' said Jamie, checking his coins as he ran.

'Thanks to that big guy. Why d'you think he helped us?'

Jamie shrugged and slowed to a walk. 'He probably doesn't like to see bullying.'

A jabbering of posh voices chattered somewhere beyond the fog. Well-to-do people were exiting a building. The words *Covent Garden Opera House* above the entrance caught Jamie's eye.

'That was a much better performance by him,' commented a middle-aged woman, wearing a white fur coat and sparkling necklace and earrings.

'Oh, yes,' replied an elderly man, through a bushy, grey moustache, 'And I think he'll be perfect taking the lead in *The Barber of Seville.*'

The man opened the door to a hackney carriage.

'That is something I must see,' said the woman, accepting his hand.

Jamie's attention fixed upon a young, well-dressed couple, giggling as they left the opera house. He admired the man's black suit and top hat, which contrasted with his white gloves and matching scarf.

The young man noticed Jamie. 'And just who do you think you are looking at?' he asked.

'Oh, don't be such a bully, Cecil,' said his companion. 'It's bad enough living on the streets, without castigation from you.'

The man snorted. 'You wouldn't be so benevolent if they snatched your purse.'

'We need the soup kitchen,' Jamie interjected. 'It's supposed to be around here, somewhere.'

The man raised his forefinger. 'Yes, I dined there a while ago, but I'm not sure where it is, now.'

The young woman sighed. 'You're such a rotter, Cecil.' She turned to Jamie, and with a smile replied, 'I'm sorry, we don't know.'

As a cab drew up beside the couple, Jamie and Todd weaved through the opera-goers to continue along the street. More departing cabs passed them.

'Dick-head,' Todd cursed, glancing over his shoulder.

They took the next turn right and came to a wide cobbled area where gas street lamps stood like dull, distant stars, barely picking out a building at the centre. Beneath the lamps, dark figures milled around.

Alarmed by the sound of dragging feet, Jamie spun round. An old hunchback approached, regarding them suspiciously with wide, staring eyes before continuing into the night. Jamie watched the fog devour the man. 'I don't like it here, Todd, I don't like all these tramps wandering about.'

'As soon as we find the soup kitchen, we'll be all right.'

'I still say we should stay in lodgings and get off these dangerous streets.'

Todd sighed. 'No. Our money won't last.'

'Why have we got to do what you want all the time?'

Todd turned sharply and pushed him. 'Go on then, go to lodgings. Like I always say, you're just a snob.' Jamie didn't move. 'Well, what you waiting for, rich boy?'

Jamie was never going to go off alone; it was scary enough when Todd was with him. 'All right, all right... the soup kitchen it is.'

They had taken only a couple of steps when Jamie stopped and peered into the mist. 'Did you hear the footsteps that time?' he whispered.

Todd looked warily about. 'It's just your imagination running wild... again! Let's ask someone where the soup kitchen is. We'll be all right, don't worry.'

Jamie stared into the grey blanket of clouds, breathing in its acrid smell. He felt unconvinced by

Todd's reassuring words. 'I don't care what you say, someone, or some*thing*, is definitely following us.'

Todd scratched his head nervously. 'Now you're really starting to freak me out.'

They set off once more, with Todd turning his head trying to detect the trailing footsteps. They passed the building at the centre of the cobbled area and before long came to a circular, cobbled junction, linking seven streets.

Evenly-spaced gas lamps glowing under thickening fog and smoke allowed Jamie to see fleeting shadowy figures. Street vendors stood in shop doorways, selling their various wares.

Todd spotted a coffee stall. 'Let's grab a coffee; the coffee-seller's bound to know where the soup kitchen is.' He smiled at the stallholder. 'Two cups of coffee, please.'

'Coming up, son.'

The stall, which supported a big copper urn, was a table draped with a white sheet, set outside The Crown public house. Accompanied by drunken singing, someone was hammering out a strangely familiar tune on a piano. The tune finished to a round of cheers, then the pianist burst into another lively rendition. The revellers roared their approval and again burst into song.

Waving his arm to indicate the numerous streets converging at the small junction, Jamie asked the coffee-seller, 'What is this place?'

'This place? Seven Dials,' replied the man, filling two cups with hot water. 'There you are.' He handed the boys their drinks. 'That's a penny.'

The stallholder's eyes widened at the silver coins in Todd's hands. Promptly, he raised his arm, seeming to wave at someone, but when Jamie looked, no one was there.

Todd asked the way to the soup kitchen but the man was distracted, looking beyond him.

He asked again.

As the coffee-seller finally gave directions, Jamie sipped his drink. 'Not bad,' he whispered to Todd, smacking his lips.

He scanned the area again. Dark figures continued to appear from the shadows and disappear again. Were they too exposed, standing by the coffee-stall under the gas lights? If only the brave Hector could be with them, then they would be safe. Where was *Hector?*

Jamie sipped some more coffee and listened to the singing within the pub.

When they'd both finished their drinks, Jamie was happy for Todd to lead the way, taking the first part of the coffee-seller's directions, a street adjacent to The Crown.

The noise from the pub had almost faded when scuffling footsteps made Jamie glance quickly back. Three apparitions came out of the smog and rapidly advanced. Three men, hats shielding their faces, grabbed Jamie and Todd roughly. 'Give us your money and we won't 'urtcha,' growled one.

'Hey, leave me alone!' Todd protested, trying vainly to resist the largest of the men.

Jamie's pockets were invaded by rummaging hands. All his coins were taken in an assault that lasted only seconds.

The muggers swaggered back towards The Crown.

Todd clenched his fist. 'We need that money back!'

Jamie's heart almost stopped when Todd marched after the men. He tagged along, knowing nothing could be gained from confronting them.

The robbers were close to the pub, and sharing out the money with the coffee-seller, when Todd challenged them. 'Give that money back,' he demanded.

'Or else - what?' replied the one with the gruff voice. He stepped close to Todd, hands on hips.

'Leave it, Todd, he'll hurt you. Come on.' Jamie tugged his friend's sleeve. 'Let's go.' Jamie could hear the thief sniggering and began to move away, but a man's voice startled him.

'Did those men just rob you?' The same suited man who had rescued them earlier now pointed a wooden staff at the robbers.

'Yes, they've taken all our money,' Todd told him.

The man passed Todd his staff and greatcoat. 'You're courting a lot of trouble tonight, aren't you? Hold these - I'll see what I can do.'

He then approached the robbers. 'I suggest you return the money you have just stolen from those boys.'

The biggest of the three men shuffled forward and without warning, struck the suited man, sending his bowler hat to the ground. 'We'll give nuffin' back,' he snarled. 'Now clear off.'

The man stroked his jaw and spoke calmly. 'I'll give you one more chance to redeem yourselves.'

The big robber bared his black teeth.

'Finish 'im off, Jack,' said the one with the gruff voice, whereupon Jack swung a fist at the man's head again. This time the suited man swerved to his right, sending Jack off balance. The swift manoeuvre enabled the man to throw a mighty left and right of his own that floored Jack, unconscious.

Jamie had never seen punches like it. This man was a hero! Then, as his rescuer stooped to retrieve his hat, the other two thugs charged at him. Jamie gave a gasp of fear and alarm for his champion, who remained crouching until both men drew close. Then, using his shoulders as a springboard, the suited man flicked one of the robbers head-first against the wall of The Crown, where he collapsed into a crumpled heap.

The third robber froze, reluctant to fight. The gathered band of on-lookers waited expectedly for him to make a move.

Just then, Todd shouted a warning to the suited man, ran up to the coffee-seller and kicked his shin hard. The man yelped, and promptly brandished a cosh.

Without giving thought to his own safety, Jamie snatched the weapon and threw it.

'Watch out!' howled Todd, as the remaining robber chose his moment, launching an attack with a kick.

The suited man turned quickly, grabbing his attacker's leg, leaving him hopping on the spot. Jamie almost laughed as the robber was spun round by the leg, all the while gathering momentum. After completing two turns the hapless robber was sent crashing into the windows of The Crown, scattering glass everywhere.

Yells and screams filled the pub and the piano abruptly stopped. The smartly dressed man ignored the chaos and retrieved the boys' money from each of the fallen men.

'That was fantastic,' Jamie cried. 'You've just beaten up three men. *And* the other man in the pub. Wow!'

'Where did you learn to fight like that?' Todd asked, grinning at their good Samaritan.

He smiled and handed the money over. 'I pick it up here and there. Let's go. The locals are getting restless.' He stopped briefly, close to the coffee-seller. 'You'd better watch out; I might come back for you.'

The coffee-seller looked down sheepishly.

'Who are you? What's your name?' Jamie asked the man as they left Seven Dials.

'My name? Just call me Bob.' He walked between them and patted their backs. 'Thanks for *your* help back there. You both showed much courage.'

'That's all right,' said Todd.

'Can you take us to the soup kitchen in Covent Garden?' asked Jamie.

'I can do better than that. Follow me.'

Bob took them through a maze of dark passageways, weaving through a heavy concentration of run-down tenements. Coal smoke from a forest of chimneys filled the alleyways and merged with the fog. Bob led the way into a quiet eating-house with three rows of finely crafted tables, covered with red-and-white check tablecloths.

He selected a quiet corner table, away from the other diners. In the well-lit establishment, Bob was revealed as clean-shaven with neatly trimmed sideburns. Minus his bowler hat, they saw that his dark hair was short but wavy.

'Now then,' said Bob cheerfully. 'Are you hungry?'

'We haven't eaten for a while,' Jamie told him.

'Good, because they do splendid lamb chops here.' He called the waitress. 'Two lamb chop dinners with potatoes and vegetables, please. Oh, and three teas.' He waited for the waitress to leave before focusing on Todd. 'So, tell me, why do you need a soup kitchen? You both look healthy and your clothes don't suggest penury.'

Who was this strange but gallant man with a kindness beyond his expectations, Jamie wondered. Why had he helped them twice? His smiling face revealed a warm person. Deciding on caution and sticking to what he told the vicar, Jamie interjected, 'We... were with my uncle, but we got separated.'

'Really?' said Bob, thoughtfully. 'So how will you find him again?'

Jamie searched for an intelligent reply but Bob's stare unnerved him. He shrugged whilst looking at Todd. 'We could try the police, I suppose.'

Bob nodded approvingly. 'Yes, you could.' Under Bob's intense gaze, Todd shuffled awkwardly in his seat. 'Is there anyone else who might help you?'

'There's an engineer we know of,' Todd mumbled.

Bob's face intensified. 'An engineer? So why don't you go and see him?'

'We don't know where he is,' Todd said.

Bob laughed. 'You know an engineer but don't know where to find him. How very odd.'

Jamie didn't like the way the conversation was going. Simon said Hector had disappeared because he was scared, and this man could be anyone, even if he had twice rescued them. 'We don't know any engineer, really,' Jamie said, sternly. 'Todd's making it all up.'

The waitress brought their teas along with a bowl of sugar. Not a word was spoken as they added sugar to their drinks. Bob stirred his tea purposefully, the spoon appearing minute in his big hand. His penetrating stare made Todd avert his eyes to the tiled floor.

Bob called to a man at the counter, drying glasses. 'Excuse me, sir. Have you any rooms for tonight?'

'Yes, I have a room. It's a shilling a night.'

Bob sipped his tea. Then, pulling out his wallet, he left the table and went to the counter.

Jamie frowned at Todd, who returned a bewildered look.

Bob came back to the table to collect his hat and staff, announcing, 'I've paid for your food and settled the room. There will be a cooked breakfast in the morning, too.' He nodded to them and said to Jamie, 'I hope you find your uncle. Goodnight.'

Jamie thanked him and, with Todd, bade him goodnight.

Todd waited until Bob had left before asking Jamie, 'What?'

'I don't know exactly, but I don't think we should tell people about Hector, especially as we know he's in hiding.'

'I just hope there's someone at the museum who will know where Hector is,' Todd said, pushing his cup away.

Jamie rubbed the bruises on his arm where the bald man with the strange beard at the museum had grabbed him so roughly. 'There's something about the museum that scares me. Those men were so... wicked.'

Todd shook his head. 'We have no other choice,' he said. 'We have to go back there.'

VI

The night's downpour had left large puddles along the cobbled streets and, beneath dark grey clouds, a bitter wind swept the city. Londoners were waking up to another cold and gloomy day.

Jamie awoke feeling rested, after a good night's sleep. Although the room was practically bare of furniture and had a damp, musty smell, his bed had been comfy. And he couldn't complain about the breakfast; eggs, bacon and mushrooms with plenty of toast. It was so good, it could have been prepared by his mum.

As they passed shops amidst the slums of St Giles, Jamie was hoping they would meet someone more friendly at the museum, who might tell them Hector's whereabouts.

Apart from the locals going about their concerns, beggars and the lame were beginning to line the muddy streets. Some sat in alleyways, others on the pavements. A queue of home-dwellers stood holding buckets, waiting their turn for water from a street pump, which was close to a small, open ditch. Jamie shuddered at the sight of what looked very much like sewage passing through it. When a now-familiar, potent smell hit his nostrils, it confirmed his fears. 'This is really unhygienic,' he whispered to Todd.

Moments later, their attention was drawn to a distressed horse in a stable-yard, where the strong smell of manure hung in the air. Three men were trying to subdue the animal, each straining on a rope, to stop it from rearing up. The stable-hands eventually calmed the horse and brought it out into the street to be harnessed to a hansom cab.

Jamie was watching them offer up the cab's shaft to the horse, when his attention was drawn to the other side of the street. A group of six shabbily dressed boys swaggered across the road, not bothering to wait for the traffic to pass. This brought a deluge of curses from a number of drivers, but the boys clearly didn't care. Although no older than 14, they maintained a confidence Jamie had never possessed; he watched them confronting an angry cab-driver and could see the truth of the saying 'safety in numbers'. That was what Jamie wanted: solidarity with others. However, by the looks on the youths' faces, he wouldn't be joining *this* gang. The leading boy wore ill-fitting clothes and a cap that was much too big for him. He glared malevolently.

Warily, Jamie studied two other boys in the group, both about the same age as himself. One sported a mop of dark-blond hair, whilst the other's colouring was very different: his white skin and hair stood out against a long, black coat and a black eye patch. But it was the boy in front who appeared the most menacing; he fixed a hard stare at Jamie's and Todd's jeans and footwear.

Todd stood firm but defensive as the boy snarled at him, 'Where you from?' When Todd didn't answer, the boy pushed him. 'I said where you from?'

Jamie knew he had to think fast. 'We're from the country, Canterbury, to be precise, and my father is in there.' He was pointing at the stables. 'And if you don't leave us alone, my father's farmhands will sort you out.'

To a round of mimicking and ridicule, Jamie led Todd into the yard, but Jamie's bluff hadn't worked, the gang lingered outside, wearing threatening scowls.

Jamie looked up at a man wearing a waistcoat and a distinctive red, silk scarf. 'Excuse me, sir,' he said, 'but is that your wagon across the road?'

When the man glanced pointedly towards the street, the gang made a hasty retreat.

'No, why?' he asked.

'Sorry, sir. I thought somebody was trying to steal it.'

Todd's grin was wide. 'Nice one, Jamie.'

Jamie took a deep breath and closed his eyes.

'We better stay here for a while,' Todd said, stepping aside, avoiding a large heap of manure.

Later, after checking that the gang had gone, Jamie and Todd set off again.

***

As they stalked the railings surrounding the British Museum, Jamie kept a watchful eye out for old weird beard. The place looked the same as when he had visited with Simon, except that the people coming to the view the exhibits today were dressed very differently.

Todd stopped. 'Well, you coming in?'

Chewing the inside of his cheek, Jamie said, 'What do we tell them? I just don't like the way that guy grabbed my arm, or the look on his face. It was evil.'

'So what are you saying? You don't want to go in there, now?'

Jamie sighed loudly, staring at the main entrance. 'Isn't there something else we could try?'

'*I don't believe this!*' Todd cried. 'We'll *never* go home.'

Jamie began muttering to himself as Todd walked to the gates and back again. 'Someone else must know Hector,' said Jamie, knowing the onslaught wouldn't be long in coming. He was right.

'Who!' Todd snarled. 'Come on, *who?* We've been to that fruitcake Colonel, there's no one left.'

'Don't call him a fruitcake, he's a military hero, you dick-head!'

'Who you calling a dick-head?' Todd grabbed Jamie's coat collars and shook him.

'Yeah, all right,' Jamie relented. Todd shoved him towards the main entrance.

Jamie was dreading another confrontation in the museum. When he reached the gates, he stopped dead as an idea struck him. Reaching for his back pocket, he brought out a notebook. 'There *is* someone who might know his whereabouts,' Jamie turned the pages while Todd waited, scowling. 'Remember Simon telling us about Hector's assistant, Catherine Wallace? And that she probably knew where Hector was hiding out? Well, I have the address where Catherine does her work: The

Science Institute, Golden Lane, Barbican. When Simon told us, I wrote it down, remember?'

Todd's tongue probed his chipped tooth and a half-smile finally appeared. 'Well done.'

Jamie broke into a broad grin. 'I think there's a chance we might be going home soon after all, Todd.' After a cautionary glance at the museum, he set off smartly, stating, 'We need a cab, quick.'

***

The traffic crawled slowly along the Strand. Black coal smoke seemed to spew from the chimneys of every building. As usual, it grasped the back of Jamie's throat and burned his nostrils.

At a busy junction, the cab came to a standstill. Four drovers, leading a flock of sheep across the road, were the cause of the snarl-up. The animals appeared frightened in the crush. Their desperate bleats grew louder, as did the angry exchanges from the impatient drivers of the stationary vehicles.

'We're well stuck and won't be moving for a while,' said Jamie. He could feel the tense atmosphere, made worse by drivers' tempers swelling. Cries of anger filled the air. A wagon tried to cut in front of their cab, only to receive a volley of abuse from their driver. Jamie jerked back in his seat as the cab's horse shot forward the few feet available, until it bumped into the horse pulling the wagon. After more jostling by the cab driver, the wagon finally gave way. Where was a bus lane when you needed one?

The sheep's fleeces almost glowed in the failing light. Jamie thought the gloom was worsening with every passing minute, yet it was only just past noon! Shops and offices were lighting-up and even some drivers had lit their lanterns.

It took a while for the cab to crawl a little further, allowing Jamie to study a huge cathedral, which he'd hitherto seen only in pictures. 'Wow! Look at that. That's St Paul's Cathedral,' he told Todd, pointing. 'I never knew it was so big.'

The pure white pillars, contrasting with the dark dome, loomed out of the swirling mists and smoke like spectral columns.

The cab turned left. Before them rose a high, dark-bricked wall, surrounding a building that reared above it like the keep of a castle. 'Newgate Prison' Jamie read on the huge iron gates.

It was another twenty minutes before the cab drew to a halt. Between trees lining the road, Jamie could see a large building with many windows and smoking chimneys, enclosed by black railings.

'Science Institute,' announced the driver.

The space in front of the Institute was completely deserted, as were the surrounding streets.

Followed by Todd, Jamie entered through two open, tall, oak doors.

'Can I assist you?' asked a uniformed man seated at a desk.

'I need to see my aunt,' Jamie told him.

'Oh yes, what's her name?'

'Catherine Wallace. It's very important.'

'Ah, I'm sorry,' said the man standing up. 'She never sees anyone, not even family, without an appointment.'

Todd stepped beside Jamie. 'But we must see her, it's very important.'

'All right. Her nephew, you say? Give me your name and I'll tell her you're here.'

Jamie raised his hand. 'Don't bother. I'm not her nephew.'

The uniformed man came from behind his desk and ushered them towards the exit. 'I don't like being lied to,' he said loudly, but once between the open doors he looked warily about the foyer. 'However, I'm... erm, retiring soon and need money,' he said in a low voice. 'So if you were to give me one sovereign, I'll make *sure* you get to see her.'

'What?' Jamie thought he must have misheard.

'Give me a sovereign and I'll let you see Miss Wallace. You look as if you come from a rich family.'

Todd brought out his change. 'What about this?'

The man laughed. 'That's nowhere near. A sovereign is £1. A gold one.'

'We haven't got £1,' Jamie told him.

The man laughed some more. 'Well, I'm afraid you can't see her.'

Once ejected from the grounds, Jamie thought hard. 'We mustn't give up, I want to go home. I've *got* to go home!' he said.

'How are we going to get in there?' Todd asked. 'Catherine's our only real chance of getting to see Hector.'

Jamie's head swirled with plans and problems. The Hawaiian holiday flashed through his mind. He recalled the brochure pictures of pure white sandy beaches and clear blue skies, a world away from this winter in which they were trapped. *'What are we going to do?'* he moaned, gazing at the leafless trees as if they might provide the answer.

'We must decide,' said Todd, 'do we try and sneak in now, or stay out here and wait for that guy to go home, then nip in and find Catherine?' He sighed loudly. 'Hey, we don't even know what this Catherine looks like.'

'I say we stay here and wait for him to go home, then sneak in.'

***

After 20 minutes, they grew steadily colder. Todd had the idea of trying to get in round the back. When they got there, the building looked exactly the same as at the front, but without the main entrance

'What now?' asked Jamie, blowing into his hands and peering through the railings.

'I can see a door,' Todd cried, his face brightening. 'Over there, look.'

Jamie nodded. 'Come on, then, let's go for it.'

They ran across the cobbled grounds to the building. Jamie looked through one of the ground-floor windows and saw an empty laboratory. They passed the lab and came to the door. It was unlocked. Todd's triumphant laugh echoed in the long corridor. Jamie told him to keep quiet. But turning the corner, they were met by the uniformed man accompanied by two men.

The man sighed angrily. 'You're in serious trouble, my lads. I saw you hiding behind the trees outside, and when you left, I knew you were going to try and get in round the back. I'm fetching the police.'

It was just the same as when the bald man had grabbed Jamie at the museum, only this time he was trying to *enter* a building. Todd, too, was jostled, and together they were escorted to the foyer.

The uniformed man had returned to his desk. Jamie studied him as he read *The Times*, whilst awaiting the arrival of the police. This was big trouble: Jamie had no idea of the penalties for trespass and he wasn't about to find out. 'You were right, what you said earlier. My family *are* rich,' Jamie announced, aware that the man was greedy. 'If you let us go, I will come back and give you *two* sovereigns to let us see Catherine.'

The man ignored him, turning the pages and reading the newspaper. Nervously, Jamie checked the main gates for the expected police. Maybe he had underestimated his greed and he was a man taking his job seriously after all.

'I said I'll give you two sovereigns.'

The man stirred and rose from the chair. He breathed in deeply, tugging his trousers up at the same time. After a brief glimpse at the man stationed outside, he said sternly, 'Very well, I'm prepared to let you go on that condition, but... ' he glared, 'if I catch you trying to sneak in again, I *will* send for the police, and furthermore, I'll have people looking out for you.' He half smiled. 'Go on then, I'll settle it with the other two, and the police when they show.'

***

Jamie decided they would have to get jobs to raise the £2. Their search for money led them half a mile from the Science Institute to a main thoroughfare, void of shops, where the traffic rumbled by, but pedestrians were few and far between. Dark brick buildings like warehouses lined the street, blending with the gun-metal grey clouds.

They had stopped for a few seconds to check their bearings, when a little girl tugged Todd's sleeve. 'What's the matter?' he asked, kneeling down to her level.

The child was no more than six and her clothes were ragged. Rubbing her eyes, she bleated, 'I've lost my mummy.'

'And we thought we had problems!' Todd said to Jamie. He turned back to the girl. 'Where was you when you last saw her?'

She pointed. 'Down there.'

'What d'you reckon, shall we help her?' Jamie nodded. 'Come on, then, little miss, let's find your mum.'

She led them about 100 yards along the street, stopping at an opening between black-brick-walled buildings. 'Down there,' she said, pointing again.

Jamie noticed a winch with a hanging chain jutting out from the top floor of what looked like a warehouse, down a narrow, cobbled passageway. Puddles gathered where the ground sloped towards the centre.

Todd picked up a stone and pulled out his catapult. 'Watch this,' he said to the girl. Taking careful aim at a horseless cart left outside an abandoned office with broken windows, he let fly a shot. But the stone flew off-course, bouncing and bobbing along the alley, out of sight. 'Whoops,' he said, pulling a wry face at the girl, but she showed no emotion. 'I'll soon get the hang of it, Jamie, you'll see.'

'You need to keep your aiming hand really still,' Jamie said.

'What do you know about catapults?' Todd snapped.

He began searching for another stone by the cart. At the same time the girl began jumping up and down, shouting, 'I'm here! I'm here!'

Suddenly, the door to the office flew open and a tall, unshaven man in a long coat and a floppy hat emerged. 'These will do!' he roared.

Two warehouse doors opposite burst open and five boys completed the ambush. Todd dropped his catapult and backed away, only to be grabbed by the man, who was now holding a knife.

VII

Jamie looked up at the tall man's big nose and protruding front teeth. His nasty grin didn't improve his features. 'Get them inside, my boys,' he growled.

Hooting with delight, the gang marched Jamie and Todd into their lair. The office was dark inside, but some daylight filtering through the open door and broken windows picked out a pile of ragged clothes on the dusty floor. There was no furniture apart from an old, soiled mattress.

Jamie offered no resistance, but Todd tried to oppose them. 'Oi, get off me!' he protested, as they bundled him against the wall.

'Soften 'im up, Scrapper,' the tall man ordered, his eyes gleaming.

One of the boys punched Todd hard in the face. Jamie shuddered as his friend fell back against the wall, blood pouring from his nose.

'No, no, no, Scrapper,' barked the man. 'How many times 'ave I told you not to hit 'em on the nose? It spoils the clobber.' He tilted Todd's head back to stem the flow of blood. At the same time, the gang started pulling at Jamie and Todd's coats. 'Now, don't worry, boys,' he said, 'just let us take your clothes and no more 'arm will come to you.'

Jamie's coat was torn off him in seconds. They must have stripped a good many unfortunates before, he thought.

Todd's coins hit the floor as his trousers were removed. His frightened expression shocked Jamie; it was a look he had never seen on Todd's face before.

'This one's got money, Mr Quick,' said one of the young robbers, picking up the coins.

'Good work, Ned,' said the man. 'What about the uvver one?'

Jamie felt their eager hands in his pockets. 'Yeah, 'e's got money an' all,' said a boy, holding up a fistful of coins.

'Even better,' said Mr Quick. Jamie lay down beside Todd; both were in just socks and underpants. 'Right, give 'em their replacements - come on, chop-chop!'

ordered Quick. When he picked up Jamie's white trainers, he inspected them closely, and tapped the rubber soles. 'Where you two from? Are you from America?'

Jamie didn't reply. He stared at Todd who, like himself, was now clad in clothing no better than rags: the trousers were wafer-thin, held up by string, and the shoes were badly scuffed.

Putting the last of their good clothes into a sack, Mr Quick said, 'You can now go.'

'What about our coats?' Todd protested, wiping blood from his face. 'We need our coats, it's freezing.'

Mr Quick feigned concern. 'I'm sorry, boys, but that's not possible. You see, I have a lot of mouths to feed; I need to keep them strong.'

Jamie - now wearing horribly short trousers - shivered with cold and fear as he and Todd shuffled from the office, whilst the gang laughed and joked their way towards the main street. His eyes blurred with tears as he watched Todd retrieve his catapult from where he'd dropped it on the ground. Up against kids like that, he thought, we're helpless.

He gave a hard sniff, 'This is what you get when you help someone. We're finished.' Shaking his head in despair, he walked to the wall, feeling every cobbled stone through the thin soles, then slid to the ground.

Todd also sniffed. 'We mustn't give up, though' he said, taking his place next to Jamie and wiping tears from his face.

Jamie was surprised to see Todd crying, and it made him feel even worse. 'Now we haven't even got any money. Didn't you say that was our only plus? We can't buy coats without money. And these bloody shoes are killing me!' Jamie hesitated before saying, 'And you're no friend, are you, really?' Todd raised his eyebrows. 'Don't look surprised, Todd. I bumped into Steve's sister a couple of days before we left for London; she said you weren't going to let me into the gang even if I did let you come to my uncle's. But I didn't mind much because we're old friends. No one would know, though. I was hoping I'd make you change your mind.'

Todd lowered his gaze to the cobbled stones and shifted awkwardly on the cold ground. 'It's... because you're rubbish at football,' he mumbled.

'Just because I can't play football, means I'm not allowed in the gang? Doesn't being friends count for something?'

'After you got rich and moved into that house, it was never the same again. Briggsy says that as well. If you'd got yourself into the school team though, you would have been allowed in the gang, I'm sure.'

'And why didn't you ever stop Wayne Carter from bullying me?'

Todd picked at the handle of the catapult. 'Carter's our best attacker, he got 39 goals last season,' he muttered. 'If I got on his back, he might have left the team, you know what he's like. He's so good, coaches from some clubs are looking at him.'

Jamie snorted with contempt. 'So what?' Jamie cried. 'I'm your friend!'

Todd swallowed hard. 'You're right, Jamie, I'm sorry, I should've helped you out.'

Silence ensued, broken only by the chattering of Jamie's teeth and Todd's occasional sniffs.

'Excuse me, darlings.'

A woman dressed in a fur coat and matching hat stood before them. 'Why are you two crying? And why is your nose bleeding?'

'We've just been robbed of our clothes and coats,' Todd told her, emitting clouds of frozen breath. 'They took our money as well.'

'You poor darlings, what a frightful thing to happen. To rob you of your coats in such inclement weather is despicable.' The woman looked up and down the alley, then said, 'Come with me.'

***

The woman led them through the back streets to a busier place, and bought them coats from one of many clothes stalls lined along the street. She then took the opportunity to clean Todd's blood-stained face at a public house en route.

'Is there anyone you know who can help you?' the woman asked.

'There is someone. Her name's Catherine, but we can't see her,' said Todd.

'I see,' replied the woman. 'Why can't you see her?'

'It's all right,' said Jamie, holding a hand up. 'We can sort it out, and thanks again for the coats.'

'Very well, but let me give you a shilling each.'

'Thanks,' said Jamie accepting his coin.

'You're welcome. Good luck my darlings, take care.'

Todd frowned, clutching his shilling, as the woman walked away. 'Why didn't you want her help?'

'We can't trust anyone in this time.'

'But she bought us these coats. And what about Bob last night? He helped us, too.'

'I know he did, but we don't know anything about these people. That lady could be out looking for boys like us to slave in a workhouse or something.'

Todd's eyebrows jumped. 'D'you think that's what she was doing?'

Jamie sighed. *'I don't know,* I was just giving you an example.'

'At least we blend in now, dressed like this,' Todd said.

Jamie ignored the remark. 'Let's find jobs,' he mumbled.

***

It was hard to imagine what jobs they were going to find, thought Jamie, before coming up with working in the stables, then Todd suggested they do what his uncle did and become removal porters. But Jamie's next suggestion was that they go back to the church and ask the vicar if he could help find them jobs. Jamie had to rely on Todd finding it, so he let him lead the way.

They were delayed at Long Lane, where a huge enclosure was being built. The whole area thrived with construction. A constant stream of carts arrived, bringing timber and bricks.

'This looks promising,' said Todd, watching as a multitude of labourers carried the building materials onto the site. 'There might be jobs going here.'

Jamie turned at the sound of whistling. A man in a black-and-white check suit, with bowler hat to match, pushed a multi-coloured handcart with a marmoset perched upon it. Gold lettering on the side of the handcart read *Mr Wiggles and his Amazing Monkey*.

Jamie and Todd couldn't take their eyes off the monkey. Jamie laughed. 'What's his name?'

'Snook,' replied the man.

'So what do you do with him, exactly, mister?' Todd asked.

'We do performances, don't we, Snook?' Mr Wiggles picked up the monkey and put it on Todd's shoulder.

Snook put one of his paws over his nose, implying that Todd had a bad odour. He then leaped onto Todd's head and stood on one leg, in a ballet pose. Todd smiled uncomfortably.

Jamie chortled.

'What's he doing?' Todd asked.

'He's pretending to be a ballet dancer on your head,' Jamie told him, laughing.

Mr Wiggles retrieved Snook and put him back on the handcart.

'What are they building here?' Jamie asked.

'It's going to be Smithfield Meat Market. Be a few years yet though, before it's finished.'

'D'you think they'd give us jobs?' Todd asked.

'Can't see why not; they're always hiring.' Mr Wiggles gave his monkey a piece of apple. 'Why don't you come to the circus, with me? I'm sure the owner would find something for you to do.'

Todd looked at Jamie. 'A circus? That would be *well* good.'

It certainly sounded more fun to Jamie than labouring.

'At least we could earn our money doing something cool,' said Todd. He stroked the monkey. 'I'd like to be an acrobat,' he said.

Mr Wiggles laughed. 'That's not easy, I can tell you. I dare say you'll probably start off as labourers. So what are your names?' he asked, and gave Snook another piece of apple.

Jamie told him their names and they all set off. After walking for five minutes they saw a large trench at the side of the road, where buildings were being demolished. 'What's happening, here?' asked Jamie. 'Look, there's a tunnel alongside the road. There's a way in.'

Mr Wiggles stopped, allowing the boys to take a look.

Todd read aloud from a large billboard: 'Metropolitan Railway.'

'Haven't you heard of the new form of transport?' Mr Wiggles asked. 'Trains that go under the ground? Sounds daft to me; only the sewers should go underground. Can't see it catching on.'

'It's the start of the London Underground,' said Jamie, softly. 'The Victorians were so clever.'

'I'd never have guessed it went this far back in time,' Todd whispered. He asked Mr Wiggles if they could take a closer look.

The showman pushed his cart to the edge, where well-to-do men in top hats and expensive-looking suits had gathered below. A number of labourers were clearing a mound of earth. Mr Wiggles snorted. 'I've read about this in the papers. They've dug a channel next to the street all the way to King's Cross Station, known as... what's it called?' He gave Snook another piece of apple. 'The "cut and cover" method, that's it. They put a roof over the top, and there you have it. I believe it goes as far as Paddington. Should soon be finished by all accounts, but you won't catch me going on it.'

'Oi!' a juvenile voice shouted.

Jamie's stomach sank; the gang they had encountered earlier, outside the stables, were spread out along the road behind them.

'Please, sir,' Jamie begged Mr Wiggles, 'you must help us. They're going to beat us up.'

The man shook his head emphatically. 'Not me, I can't do that. I don't get involved with street gangs; right little urchins they can be, make no mistake.' And with that, he was off, calling back to them, 'I'm sorry, but I have to go.'

'Where's your dad's farmhands now?' said the same boy who had pushed Todd earlier.

Jamie looked frantically for an escape route, hoping Todd was doing the same, but the approaching gang now had both ends of the street cut off. It was Todd who took drastic action: grabbing Jamie's arm and leading him to the edge of the construction site, where an iron ladder fixed to the wall led all the way down to the bottom.

The gang's ringleader yelled at his mates to get them.

As Jamie and Todd descended the ladder, they were pelted with stones. The gang were still throwing stones as the two of them ran across the site, dodging the businessmen and ignoring an order to stop.

Jamie sprinted into the tunnel.

Almost at once they were shrouded in total darkness. Their footsteps, as well as those of pursuing workmen, echoed off the walls.

'I can't go on, Todd, I'm scared.' Jamie recoiled from the blackness bearing in on him.

'We mustn't give up, keep going,' Todd's voice echoed.

Jamie felt Todd's reassuring hand clasp his arm; it gave him the courage to continue. He was relieved to hear the labourers' footsteps fade, and it seemed safe to stop running.

'What now?' Jamie said, his voice unsteady, bouncing of the walls.

'At least we haven't been caught.'

'Yet.'

'Don't be so negative.'

'I don't like this, Todd. We could be down here for miles.' He stared into the blackness and reached out a hand, touching Todd for reassurance.

'We mustn't panic.'

'I want to get out.' Jamie's breathing quickened. 'Let's go back, Todd.'

Todd grabbed at him. 'We can't go back, they'll get the police.'

Jamie's legs felt weak and a foreboding set in. He stopped.

'Come on,' Todd urged, tugging his arm.

'I... I can't.'

Todd didn't reply.

Silence.

Jamie waited for Todd, but heard only silence. 'Todd?' No answer. 'Todd, where are you? Don't muck around!' Jamie probed with clutching hands but met only a black emptiness. What had happened to Todd? 'Oh, my God,' Jamie cried. 'Todd!'

Todd's steady voice came from the far wall. 'Are you ready, now?'

'That's not funny!'

'It wasn't meant to be.' Todd came close. 'You have a choice; either we stay down here or we try and get out.'

After groping their way for another five uncertain minutes, the two boys found salvation: a ladder and a shaft of daylight from a maintenance hatch above.

They emerged onto the street, close to the wheels of passing horse-driven carts and carriages. As Todd closed the hatch, they heard a boy's voice shouting, 'There they are!'

'I don't bloody believe this!' Jamie shouted, scrambling to his feet.

The chase was back on with the group of six boys shouting threats.

Todd pointed to a stationary omnibus, off-loading several passengers. 'We can make that, come on.'

Together they ran to the vehicle. Its uniformed conductor stood on the road helping an elderly lady dismount, then he leapt onto a small iron platform and banged on the side-panelling, signalling the driver to move. The vehicle's two horses broke into a trot after Jamie and Todd had clambered on board. It was a tight squeeze on the platform and, as they grabbed the handrails, the conductor scowled at them.

Jamie realised that everyone on the lower deck was looking at them. Most were women who wore colourful dresses under their heavy coats, and flamboyant hats. He exchanged a long stare with a girl of about eight, who fiddled with a rag doll.

'Are you going to pay, or am I going to throw you off?' the conductor asked.

After Jamie received change from the shilling he'd been given, they were directed to the open, top deck where male passengers only were sitting on bench-seats. Jamie took his seat smiling, having escaped the gang, but Todd's odd behaviour baffled him; he remained standing, looking down at the street below.

'What's wrong?' Jamie asked.

'That's really weird,' said Todd.

'What is?'

'I just saw that guy who helped us last night. You know, Bob.'

'So?'

The omnibus started to slow down.

'He looked shocked, staring up at me,' Todd said. 'But the really weird thing is... he was with that woman in the fur hat and coat.'

That did seem strange, Jamie agreed. His mind paid little attention to the loud commotion down below as the omnibus stopped. 'You're right, that *is* weird.'

'You're not coming on board, now clear off!' the conductor was heard to shout below.

His words were met with a barrage of hostile juvenile voices. Jamie looked towards the back of the omnibus, aghast to see the boy with the dirty face appear. 'Gotcha!' the boy yelled.

VIII

The bus had long since disappeared. The conductor had ordered all boys off regardless of who was causing the trouble. He might as well have delivered them into the hands of the mob, Jamie thought, surveying the deserted, muddy alleyway with alarm.

'So where's your farver's farmhands now?' snarled the boy who had been so threatening before.

The rest of the gang glared malevolently.

Jamie feared a serious beating. Where was Bob, coming to their rescue? This time they were alone.

The gang all clenched their fists as if at a signal. 'Get 'em!' cried one large youth.

'Wait!' Jamie screamed. Amazingly, the gang stopped, as if he had something important to say. He spoke quickly. 'Why do you want to beat us up? What have we done to you? Six against two isn't fair, is it? Give us a chance.'

'Wotcha mean?' asked the mouthy boy.

'Why can't we make things fair? You, fight one of us.'

'All right then,' said the boy accepting the challenge. 'Which one of ya am I going to fight?'

Jamie pointed to Todd. 'Him.'

Todd gasped and, as the mouthy boy stepped back, allowing his gang to remove his coat, demanded, 'What are you playing at, Jamie? It's your idea, so why ain't you fighting him?'

'Because you're the boxer, aren't you? You keep telling me how good you are, so here's your chance to show me.'

'But I've only been five times,' Todd replied, sizing up his opponent, who was now stripped for action.

'You've changed your tune,' Jamie teased, massaging Todd's shoulders, trainer-style. 'A little while ago you could beat anyone. Listen, Todd, I've just saved us from a bad beating – '

Todd shrugged off Jamie's hands. 'You mean you've saved *yourself* from a beating.'

Jamie watched the gang psyching up their friend for the fight. 'If you can put up a good fight, I think we'll be

OK.' Jamie ignored Todd's look of contempt. 'You're fighting for the 21st Century here, just think of that. And for the Riverside Posse.'

'I think you're enjoying this,' said Todd, taking off his coat.

'I'm not, Todd. I'm well behind you.'

'Come on, then.' The mouthy one stood ready with his shirtsleeves rolled up.

Jamie patted Todd's back. 'Good luck,' he said.

'Get 'im, Billy!' shouted the others.

Billy came at Todd with fists swinging. One caught him on the side of the head. Todd stepped back, but the onslaught continued; Billy connected with two more punches to his face.

The gang yelled with delight, relishing the sight of their friend taking control and hitting Todd at will. After the initial barrage, and to Jamie's relief, Todd began to use some of his defensive skills, dodging first to his left, then his right. The manoeuvre left Billy wide open for Todd to hit him on the chin with a jolting left jab. Billy wobbled and his gang members froze, horrified to see their hero take a flurry of blows.

'Go on, Todd!' Jamie shouted, forgetting the gang's presence. He could hardly believe it; Todd had taken control, with Billy now cowering.

Billy crouched, avoiding Todd's punches, and launched a fresh attack. He ran at Todd, grabbing his midriff and sending them both crashing to the muddy ground. In the ensuing grapple, Billy gained the advantage, squeezing Todd's neck in a headlock. The gang started to cheer again and Todd's face reddened under pressure on his windpipe. He twisted sharply to deliver a number of punches to Billy's stomach. By now, both boys were tiring. Billy's grip loosened under the onslaught of Todd's heavy blows, but before Todd could capitalise on this, Billy grabbed a handful of mud, smeared it into his opponent's eyes, and began hitting him in the face.

The gang screamed in triumph.

'That's enough, you win!' A worried Jamie intervened.

Billy stood up, gulping in air, whilst Todd remained on the ground, wiping the mud from his face.

'Good fight,' said the gang member, offering his hand.

Todd rubbed his bruised face.

'What's your names?' Billy asked.

Jamie told them.

Billy, licking blood from his lip, put on his cap and coat. 'I'm Billy.' He pointed at his friend with the untidy blond hair. ''e's Joe, and that's Patch - well, you can see why we call 'im that.'

Jamie had never come across anyone like Patch before, and the boy's red eye baffled him.

Billy pointed to the boy with a swarthy complexion. 'And that's Luigi.' To the two younger gang members he said, 'Youse can go. We'll meet up later. Luigi, go wiv 'em.' He frowned at Jamie and Todd. 'Weren't youse dressed in better clobber earlier?'

Todd nodded. 'We was robbed of our clothes not long before you caught up with us. They took our money as well.'

Billy grinned. 'D'you want to join us? We're going to Ludgate Street to meet the two o'clock.'

'What's the two o'clock?' Jamie asked.

Billy laughed. 'Where you two from?'

'Canterbury,' Jamie replied, a mite embarrassed.

'Jamie's the rich boy, but not me, though,' Todd joked, making Jamie cringe.

'The two o'clock is a very important meeting and I would be 'appy if you came wiv us. There might be a chance for you to get some money back.'

Jamie drew Todd aside. 'You did well fighting him,' he said. 'I can't believe you almost mashed him up, but I don't think it's a good idea to go with them.'

Todd used his coat-sleeve to wipe the last of the mud from his face. 'Didn't you hear him? We might get some money. We have to eat, Jamie. *And* we need money to have a chance to see Catherine, remember?'

'I know, but I'm not sure about this. I reckon if we were to walk away now, they'd let us go.'

Todd gazed briefly at Billy. 'Maybe - but we still need money, don't we? Let's just go with them for a while. We could do with some friends, too.'

Jamie pondered. Tagging along with Billy and his friends did appeal and he had always wanted to join a gang, so here was his chance. 'All right, but I bet this two o'clock is bad news. I don't want to end up in a Victorian prison.'

***

Jamie trailed the group approaching a busy junction. He saw Todd pick up a smooth, rounded pebble from the kerb and put it in his pocket.

'Wotcha do that for?' asked Billy.

Todd showed him his catapult. 'I collect stones for this.'

Billy took it and asked for a stone. 'What can I go for?' he muttered, looking around the busy street.

He selected a pile of coal sacks stacked against the wall of a candlemaker's on the other side of the street.

Pulling back the elastic, he waited for a gap in the passing traffic. Todd laughed at Billy's nerve but Jamie could see that passers-by were getting annoyed. What if someone called the police?

Billy released the missile but missed the sacks by some distance. The stone bounced off the pavement and ricocheted against the shop wall before thudding loudly into the side of a passing carriage.

'Scarper!' cried Billy, laughing as he ran.

Jamie had no choice but to hurry after them, dodging agitated pedestrians. Billy was laughing as he led the way, but his jovial mood soon vanished. He slowed to a jog at the busy junction and raised his arm, signalling his followers to halt. 'Over there, look!'

A smartly dressed, overweight man was paying off a hansom cab driver outside an accountant's office on the corner of Fleet Street. His expensive, Lincoln-green coat, matching trousers and shiny, black top hat suggested opulence. The red-faced city gent joked with the driver, holding his silver-topped cane under his arm, as he dug in a small pouch for coins.

'Stand 'ere and look out for Peelers,' Billy commanded.

'What are Peelers?' Jamie asked, confused.

Billy frowned back. 'The police, you muttonhead.'

Jamie beckoned Todd away from the others. 'What are we getting caught up in?' he whispered. 'We're going to be involved in a mugging, and it's not like the place is deserted.'

Todd bit on his bottom lip. 'We're not exactly spoilt for choice and we've been through a lot lately. All we have to do is watch out for the cops,' he said.

'I can't do this.' Jamie sighed before walking away and leaning against a shop window. Any passer-by could realise what they were doing at any moment, and he spotted an office clerk leaning out of a window on the first floor of a building opposite.

As he watched the busy crossroads, Jamie found himself thinking about the worst thing he had ever done; knocking on someone's door and then running away. This was much more serious. He gnawed anxiously at a fingernail while he watched Todd acting as look-out as Billy and Joe closed in on their prey like hunting-dogs. Patch had already gone on ahead, as another lookout.

Joe and Billy now stood either end of the cab, waiting for their chance. The red-faced businessman handed over the fare and bade farewell to the driver. Billy stood behind the horse, watching the man returning the pouch to his back pocket.

Jamie walked over to Todd. 'I suppose if I was in the Riverside Posse, I'd have to do daring things,' he said.

Todd smiled nervously.

Billy and Joe made their move. The man had almost reached the doorway only to be blocked by Joe. This seemed to annoy him. He waited impatiently for Joe to move aside and it was then that Billy pounced. On lifting the man's coat-tail, he slid out the pouch, alerting his overweight victim.

'Hey!' the man cried, grabbing his back pocket. 'I've been robbed! Stop, thief! Somebody stop them!'

Billy and Joe bolted from the spot, as did Patch, Todd and Jamie.

Jamie soon overtook Todd, weaving along the crowded pavement. Breathing in the smoke made his lungs feel as if they were on fire.

It seemed for now that they'd got away with it.

Billy and his two friends dived into a side street.

A panting Todd caught up with Jamie. 'That were cool, weren't it?'

By the time they turned the corner, they were down to a brisk walk. Jamie coughed, inhaling the suffocating smoke. 'I don't think we should stay with them any longer, Todd. I can see us getting caught.'

Todd looked doubtful. After much deliberation, he spoke between panting and coughing. 'We'll get paid out, then leave them, yeah?' He cupped his hand over his mouth. 'I can't stand this smoke, can you?' he moaned.

Billy smiled broadly as they approached him. 'What are you two talking about?' he asked.

'The smoke, it chokes, doesn't it?' Todd replied.

Billy laughed. 'You're in the big city now, you country bumpkins. He set off with them and said, 'You did well.' He then led the way into a busy, decrepit-looking eating house, its windows wet with condensation due to a roaring fire and the hot, steamy kitchen.

They took their seats at the only available table, amongst labourers, porters and cab drivers. The room was clouded in thick tobacco smoke, as stagnant as the smog outside. The owner, a thickset man, whipped a dish-cloth over his shoulder and came to their table to ask, harshly, 'What d'you want?'

'Five teas,' said Billy.

'Give me a tanner, first,' the man said, holding out his hand.

Billy paused, looking at each of the boys before discreetly opening the stolen pouch. The proprietor waited impatiently and glowered at Billy as he carefully selected the right coinage. 'There you are, my good man,' he said in a would-be posh accent.

The man snatched the money. 'Don't come it.'

Joe and Patch sniggered along with Todd when the owner left the table, but Jamie was too worried about the trouble they were in to join in.

Billy cautiously opened the pouch again, making sure they weren't being watched. 'I fink we've done well, lads,' he announced, grinning. He emptied the coins onto the table, shielding them with his other hand.

Joe and Patch both stared intently. Their eyes widened when Billy pulled four gold coins from the heap.

'Sovereigns,' Joe whispered with glee.

Billy slid one sovereign to each of his friends, who eagerly pocketed them, and took one for himself. ''enry can have the uvver one.'

'Who's Henry?' asked Todd.

''Enry 'Olton, the leader of the gang we're in. We 'ave to earn our stay by doing fings like this, but one day we're going to start our own gang, ain't we?' Joe and Patch nodded enthusiastically. 'You never know, you two could be in it.'

'Yeah!' Todd's now-glittering eyes filled Jamie with dread, although Billy's mention of forming a gang did raise his own curiosity. His wish to be in a gang was there for the taking, even if it was only to be until they raised the £2 to see Catherine.

Jamie hesitated before asking Billy, 'Why are you in a gang?'

'For survival, my friend. I'm surprised you two ain't in one.'

Todd piped up excitedly. 'I'm in a gang... in Canterbury.'

Billy sniggered. 'Who's in it, a bunch of rabbits?'

Everyone around the table, including Jamie, burst out laughing.

Todd lowered his gaze and Billy started to quickly sort out the rest of the coins, giving some silver and copper ones to Joe and Patch. Two half-crowns were pushed towards Todd and Jamie. 'That's for youse.'

Todd picked up the large coins. 'Thanks.' He examined the unfamiliar money. 'How many of these make £1, Billy?'

Billy stared at him. 'Eight, of course. You two are strange.'

'We only need 14 more of these, Jamie,' Todd said.

'Why d'you need £2?' Billy asked.

Jamie gave Todd a warning look, just as Joe joked, 'No wonder that man made such a fuss when we took his money.'

Jamie sat quietly watching Todd and the others laughing and ribbing each other. Hadn't Todd said they'd get their share then leave Billy? So why was he so keen to join the gang?

Billy fastened the pouch. ''enry can 'ave the rest.'

The big café-owner approached their table with their teas on a tray. Billy looked at a large clock on the wall and stood up. 'We don't want those now; we've got to go somewhere.'

***

Avoiding the busy junction, Billy navigated through a maze of back alleys until they emerged under the shadow of St Paul's. Jamie recognised the street from earlier when they had passed through in the cab.

He plucked at Todd's sleeve as they were buffeted amidst the jostling crowds. 'I thought we were going to leave them after we got paid out?' Todd didn't reply. 'And what *does* Billy mean by meeting the two o'clock?' Jamie made sure they were out of earshot. 'Let's leave them, Todd, while we still have a chance. If we stay with this lot we're going to get caught doing something bad.'

Todd brought out his half-crown. 'We only need 14 more of these and we can get to see Catherine. It shouldn't take that long to get the money.'

Jamie looked at the big silver coin in Todd's hand. What he said was true, but how long could they go on breaking the law before being captured?

Billy interrupted Jamie's thoughts by stopping outside a hat shop, watch in hand. 'Ten minutes to two,' he announced, staring across the street to a coaching inn.

A carriage entrance to a courtyard also gave access to accommodation and stables. Billy's gaze remained fixed on the inn. 'Any time now, the coach from Cambridge will be in. When it comes, Patch will wait at Watling Street, and you two will stand ivver side of that entrance over there, watching out for Peelers. If you see any, tell us, quick. Yeah? When the coach is in the courtyard, me and Joe will wait for the right moment to snatch a case.' Billy's nonchalance scared Jamie. 'Me or Joe, whoever gets the case, will run to Watling Street and 'and it to Patch. You two follow the one who ain't got the case.'

'He makes it sound so easy,' Jamie whispered to Todd. 'But I'm scared. If we get caught, then what...?'

'We won't!' said Todd. 'They know what they're doing.'

A police Black Maria with slits in the sides of its iron body and pulled by four huge horses, rumbled by slowly in the column of traffic. The policemen aboard glared down at the boys; Jamie shuddered and peeled away.

'Jamie, come back,' called Todd, jogging to catch him up. 'Where you going?'

'Away from these crooks,' Jamie snapped. 'We're going to finish up in jail and that'll be the end of us. We'll be stuck in this time forever.'

'I know how you feel, but let's do this one last thing,' Todd pleaded.

'And then it will be something else.' Jamie shook his head.

'I thought you wanted to be in a gang. Here's your chance.'

Jamie sighed forcefully. 'That's ridiculous, and you know it. You wouldn't do anything like this in the Riverside Posse, would you?' Todd didn't answer; he just stared at Jamie without blinking. 'You mean you *have* stolen things with them?'

'You know the convenience store in Sutton Street, the one where the owner died last month? Not long after he died, me, Turbo and Dan broke in one night and took loads of stuff. Me mum was well happy; she's still using all the washing powder I got her. Remember the day we came to school with all them chocolate bars? They were from the shop, too.'

Jamie remembered all too well: he'd not been given one! That's not right, Todd.'

Todd snorted. 'To get into the Riverside Posse you'd have had to steal something. It's usually from Grace's

Store: one of us distracts her while the other nicks the sweets.'

'But she's an old woman, I like Gracie,' said Jamie, remembering how she always gave him a smile and asked how his family were.

Todd paused. 'Look, for the first time since we've been here, I feel I belong to something, don't you? Being with them can teach us about this time, *and* protect us from gangs who'd nick our clothes. We've got to wise up, if we're going to survive.'

'Yeah, but I don't want to break the law, not here, anyway. We should have gone with that guy and joined the circus.'

Billy came over to them and slapped Todd's back. 'Don't worry, now that the patrol 'as passed we should be all right. Oh, and by the way, 'ere comes the two o'clock.'

Jamie watched as the Cambridge-to-London coach slowly approached them, then tensed as Patch left to take up his position. Billy nodded for him and Todd to take up their positions.

As he crossed the road, scraping his feet, Jamie could feel his energy draining away. He wanted to be sick.

Pulled by four steaming horses, the big coach drew nearer. It was packed with passengers who sat inside as well as up on top. Jamie peered closely at them as the Star Company vehicle passed by him. Why was he doing this? How had he been talked into robbing innocent people?

He looked up at the driver, whose huge frame bulged beneath a heavy greatcoat, and the guard who sat at the back of the coach. As they approached the courtyard, the guard climbed down from the roof and stood at one side of the coach, stopping the oncoming traffic, giving the driver the wide swing needed to enter.

As they drew to a stop, the horses' hooves echoed in the courtyard, a sound followed at once by that of disembarking passengers. They took their time.

Despite the cold air, sweat trickled down Jamie's back. He watched Billy talking intently to Joe, still on the other side of the road but with a clear view of the coach; it seemed that he was planning every detail.

Todd called to Jamie in a low voice. 'How are we supposed to spot the cops in all this lot?'

Jamie ignored the question. He couldn't see Billy and Joe now, because a cart with a giant bowler hat on the back, was in the way. He read the large white letters on the side-panelling: *Cuthbert's Headgear, hats for all occasions.* He looked to his right, checking for police vehicles in the long column of traffic which stacked all the way back to Fleet Street and beyond. He looked left: Billy and Joe strode out across the road; Jamie's anxious eyes followed them into the courtyard.

The passengers were now in the coach house, while their luggage was being unloaded. The guard, back on the roof of the coach, handed the cases down to the driver, who'd taken off his greatcoat.

'D'you want any 'elp, mister?' asked Billy, his eyes trained on the luggage.

'No! Get lost,' snapped the driver, not bothering to look at him.

At that rebuke, Billy nodded to Joe and made for the pile of luggage. Joe slammed into the driver, enabling Billy to grab a case, but the driver recovered his balance swiftly and grabbed Billy by the arm. Joe tried to rescue his friend by kicking the man, repeatedly and hard, on the back of the leg, but the driver held on to him, and shouted to the guard for help.

Billy, still holding the case, was being roughly shaken. Jamie stood in the entrance, watching it all go horribly wrong.

IX

'Give me the catapult and some stones!' Jamie shouted urgently.

Todd was quick to respond and Jamie loaded the weapon as he ran into the courtyard. The driver had his back to them and was still wrestling with Billy, who was struggling wildly. Jamie took quick aim and released a stone at full power, and scored a direct hit on the man's buttocks. He froze, then let out a roar.

Billy broke free and made his escape with the case, but the guard immediately confronted him. Jamie had already reloaded: he fired a stone at the man's knees. There was a sickening crack, followed by the guard crashing to the ground. He lay writhing on the cobbles.

Suddenly, two stable-hands raced into the courtyard, alarmed by the ensuing robbery, but Jamie was fast reloading and had the elastic pulled back at full stretch, aimed right at them. He ordered them to the ground. When they saw the agony the driver and guard were in, they reluctantly obeyed.

Jamie had total control; he ruled for those few seconds - and what a feeling! But he knew not to wait around; he spun on his heels and made for the entrance, where Billy, Joe and Todd were waiting.

The getaway was on!

Billy ran on the north side of the street, heading for the handover with Patch. Todd and Jamie followed Joe, crossing the road, dodging the traffic, taking the first right turn, and then a combination of lefts and rights, until a foggy view of the River Thames appeared. Jamie could discern the merchant steamships and sailing boats, moving like silent ghost ships.

'I can't believe what you did back there,' Joe said. 'I saw it all.' He shook his head and leaned on a wall. 'I've never seen anyfing like it.'

'Or me,' said Todd, studying his friend closely. 'How are you so good with the catapult, Jamie?'

Jamie turned from the river and tossed the catapult away. Todd caught it. 'I've been practising for ages with my own catapult, over at Meadow Fields after school. Looks like it paid off, eh?' He leaned close to Todd's ear. 'Nothing's going to stop me from getting back; I'm going on that holiday to Hawaii.' Todd laughed uncertainly. Grinning shamefacedly, Jamie admitted, 'I thought it was fun too, picking them men off.'

'Jamie, you 24-carat, priceless so-and-so.' Billy walked towards them with his usual swagger and a broad smile. Playfully, he punched Jamie in the stomach. 'Where on erf did you ever learn to aim like that?'

Jamie couldn't hide his grin. 'Practice, I suppose.'

'The way them men fell. Wait till ''enry 'ears about it.'

'When are we going to see Henry?' Todd asked.

'When it's dark.' Billy looked up at the swirling grey mists. 'Won't be long now. We'll wait for Patch and take a slow walk back and try out that new gin palace at Charing Cross. It's gonna be real blaggin' wevver tonight.'

***

It was five o'clock in the evening when Jamie and Todd followed the boys near Seven Dials. Jamie got another whiff of alcohol from Billy's breath and it took him back to the gin palace with its sculptured metal ceiling and walls covered with over-elaborate, coloured ceramic tiles. Who would believe such places had ever existed, or the number of young children who got blazingly drunk in them?

The darkness and thick fog almost hid the sack containing the stolen case, draped over Patch's shoulder. They all walked in silence until Jamie realised that Billy and his friends had stopped.

'Be careful,' Billy advised, in a whisper.

With one foot, Jamie probed cautiously for the top of a step, then descended, clutching an iron handrail. Shrouded in complete darkness, he had visions of entering Hell, where Henry Holton was the Devil and the rest of the gang his demons.

At the bottom of the steps, Billy pushed past him. 'What are you doing?' Jamie whispered.

'There's a chain sticking out of the wall at the bottom of the door,' replied Billy, who was now crouching. 'I pulled it free times, giving the code for them to come.'

Suddenly, an opening appeared at eye-level, as a brick was pulled from the inside of the wall. 'Who is it?' challenged a youth's voice, through the gap.

'It's Billy. Let us in.'

A youth opened the door. He held an oil lamp that picked out the chain running along the wall and beyond. Billy spoke quietly as they trailed behind the teenager with the lamp. "Is name's 'Awk. They call 'im that for 'is skill at picking pockets, so keep 'old of yer 'alf-crowns.'

Jamie and Todd were taken deeper, through what looked like storage rooms, until they reached a door with a dull glimmer of light shining beneath it. Hawk opened the door.

Jamie's first impression was of the many staring eyes from the side walls. An overpowering, mouldy odour hung in the air, mixed with a subtle whiff of roasting chickens. The smell of them cooking made him realise just how hungry he was.

Many boys and several young girls, half-hidden in the semi-darkness, sat on boxes or on the cold floor. Billy said they were strays and orphans who would rather be in the gang than on the streets or slaving away in a workhouse.

As Jamie shuffled forward, he discovered that columns either side of the underground room were supporting the low ceiling. At the far end of the room, beneath three oil lamps, a scruffy-looking group of young men and boys sat around a desk - presumably a leftover from the business that had once occupied this place.

Jamie stayed close to Todd, accompanied by Billy and the other two. The chickens were cooking on spits near the end wall, where shadowy figures moved around.

Henry Holton, the young and powerfully built gang-leader, sat in a big leather chair, hands clasped together. Blond hair pulled back into a ponytail framed his stern face.

Jamie found himself directly under the light, conspicuous in the glare. Henry picked up a bottle of rum and leaned forward. He stared menacingly at them all: Patch, Billy, Joe, Todd and Jamie.

Patch and Billy placed their booty on the desk. The stolen case was taken for inspection.

Before raising the bottle to his lips, Henry asked in a harsh voice, 'Who are these wiv ya, Bill?'

Billy spoke eagerly. 'We met these two today, and if it wasn't for Jamie 'ere wiv 'is sling-shot, we would never 'ave got the case. And I would 'ave been in deep lumber, make no mistake.'

Flanked by his mainstays, Henry drank the rum. Jamie thought he looked like a general surrounded by his officers. One of the boys sitting on the edge of the desk was no more than 16, yet he smoked a long-stemmed pipe and wore a deerstalker hat.

Another, older boy at the desk wore a red bandana and a gold earring; his swarthy complexion hinted at a gypsy origin.

Henry leant back in the chair and wiped his mouth with the back of his hand. 'So you bring someone in wiv a talent, at last?'

Billy was off again. 'Yeah, when I snatched the case, the driver, 'e grabbed me. That's when Jamie shot 'im up the bum.' There were ripples of laughter among the younger members. 'Then the guard started but Jamie, he shot 'im an' all. In the leg he got 'im, but then more blokes came. That's when Jamie told 'em to get on the ground.'

Henry swallowed some more rum, nodding approvingly. He beckoned Jamie closer. 'I like what I 'ear, Jamie. You see, I like to surroun' myself wiv talent. I've got pickpockets, real good blaggers, lock-pickers, good brawlers. But someone good wiv the sling-shot, that can 'ave so many advantages. You never know, give it a while and you too could 'ave a seat at my desk.' He viewed Todd sceptically. 'And what about you, got any skills?'

Todd stood silent, fiddling with his hands. After a pause he offered, 'I'm skilful with a football.'

Billy shook his head. Everyone else around the desk stared blankly at Todd, but Henry just laughed, which started everyone else off. The fearsome leader was highly amused. 'I'm skilful wiv a football,' he repeated, and laughed some more.

The atmosphere lifted. Henry turned to a hefty young black man with a shiny bald head. 'I don't need you as second-in-command, Zad, I've got someone skilful wiv a football.'

Zad rumbled with merriment.

Henry stood up and skirted the desk. 'I can see it now, the Peelers come and you kick footballs at 'em.' He mimed a kick.

'They could trip over the balls,' the bandana-wearer suggested.

The youth with the pipe provided another idea: 'Or he could kick a ball at a window and so make an entry.'

'Yes, Swiper, I like it,' said Henry, grinning.

There were hoots of hysteria; even Jamie was laughing heartily. And Todd, who until now had remained sombre, nervously taking the flak, began to laugh, too.

Henry returned to his chair. 'What's your name?'

'Todd,' Todd muttered meekly.

A middle-aged woman, as blonde as Henry, entered the room. 'What's so funny?' she asked, nearing the desk with an air of confidence. Henry told her about the new recruits. Jamie wilted under her close scrutiny. Although her clothes were shabby, her hands weren't. She stroked Jamie's face gently, using fingers with long, manicured nails. Everyone observed her inspection of him in silence. 'Such a healthy and clean complexion,' she murmured. Holding Jamie's chin softly, the woman asked, 'Where are you two from?'

'Canterbury.' Jamie took the courage to look into her blue eyes, adding, 'We're lost, Miss. We came to London with my uncle and got separated.'

The woman looked Jamie up and down and said, 'You're dressed like street urchins, but if you've come from Canterbury to London, you must 'ave money.'

'Todd and I were robbed of our clothes, earlier today,' Jamie told her.

She turned to Henry and said, in a loud and angry voice, 'Your 'new recruits' should be back in Canterbury!'

'Shut up,' Henry replied abruptly.

'You might be in charge 'ere, but you're still my son,' she snapped. 'If your farvver was alive to 'ear that, 'e would 'ave tanned your backside. You don't tell me to shut up.'

Henry's hard expression remained. 'I make the decisions 'ere, so they're staying put. Now please... sit down.'

Henry waited for his mother to sit close by then picked up the stolen pouch and spoke to Billy. 'So where d'you lift this?'

'I took it from a fatty in Fleet Street.'

Henry loosened the cord and let the copper and silver coins fall out onto the desktop. 'Not bad, Bill, not bad.' The gang-leader pocketed the sovereign. He then pushed five shillings - one for each boy - to the edge of the desk.

Jamie eyed his second reward of the day and couldn't help feeling pleased with himself; it was more money towards their Catherine fund. He watched the gang discreetly, approving of the way they all worked for one another. He could see they were not banded together because they preferred this life of crime, but because there was no other way. In these days, there was no welfare and nothing like the benefits system that Todd's mum enjoyed as a single parent. And now the glaring difference between this gang and the

Riverside Posse could be seen: Todd's gang didn't *have* to exist.

Billy collected his reward first, followed by Patch and Joe. When Jamie picked up his coin, Henry pushed another two shillings in his direction. 'You can 'ave a bonus, Jamie.'

'Thanks,' said Jamie picking up the extra money. He started to smile, but then bit his lip. Was he *really* comfortable at being rewarded for theft?

Billy patted him on the back. 'It's not every day 'enry gives a bonus,' he said.

'It's 'ardly any day, young Bill,' Henry corrected him. He spoke to the youth in the bandana at the edge of the desk. 'Get the box, Philip.'

Philip headed off to the end of the room, passing the roasting chickens, and came back with a wooden strongbox. As he opened it, Henry called to the boys sorting through the case. 'Anyfink of value?' A reply revealed that there were some good clothes and footwear, and that it was a good case.

Henry nodded approvingly and deposited the stolen coins in the strongbox. He handed it back to Philip and focused on Jamie. 'Let me see 'ow good you are wiv the sling-shot.'

Todd handed Jamie the catapult and some stones, and merged into the shadows to watch.

Billy found an empty rum bottle, took it to the other end of the room and placed it on a barrel. Then he lifted a lamp, and held it high, illuminating the target.

Jamie nodded to himself confidently. He could hit it easily. He raised the loaded catapult and slowly pulled back the elastic, lining the bottle up within the vee of the implement. The room fell silent. He fired the stone. Instantly, the sound of smashing glass rang out.

There was a round of applause from the youngsters along the walls. Jamie smiled triumphantly.

When he looked at Henry, the gang-leader was nodding, as were many of the boys. 'Very good, Jamie,' came his gruff praise. He pointed a thumb over his shoulder. 'Go and 'ave somefing to eat. You too, Todd. And Jamie, after you've eaten, come and take a seat at the desk.'

***

Todd sat by himself on a barrel, away from everyone else in the hideout. Things were quiet. The flame from a tallow candle flickered violently in cross-currents of cold air that swept the dank room; its glow revealed Todd's miserable face; Jamie had sat most of the night with Henry and his mainstays. It was 15 minutes to midnight.

Jamie left the desk and strolled over to Todd.

'What you doing standing with me?' asked Todd. 'I thought I weren't good enough any more.'

Jamie held back a smile. Todd didn't know how satisfying it felt to be the one favoured by the gang. How things had changed regarding the Riverside Posse! 'Henry asked me to sit with him, Todd. Was I supposed to refuse? Besides, he's the boss, so we need to - '

Todd interrupted with a half-hearted laugh, and said sourly, 'And you're like some super-hero with the catapult to them young kids. I saw you earlier, giving it large.'

Jamie smiled. 'What's up? Don't you like me getting all the attention? Makes a change, don't you think?'

Todd looked down at his fumbling hands. 'I've been thinking about what I'd miss if we don't make it back to our time. What would you miss most?'

'But we *are* going to make it back,' Jamie said.

'But if we don't.'

Jamie paused. 'You know - my family... and that holiday in Hawaii.' He smiled ruefully. 'And proper toilet paper.'

Todd hesitated. 'That reminds me, I had the trots real bad earlier, it was like water, and my stomach feels really strange.'

'You must have caught a bug or something.'

Todd nodded. 'That's what I thought.'

'What about you, what would you miss?'

'My family as well and all my computer games.' Jamie agreed, nodding emphatically. 'And football,' Todd added. 'Which reminds me; you'd be in the Posse now, no sweat, as you're so cool with the catapult. You're much better than Steve.' He laughed ruefully. 'We could have done with you, fighting that gang with the air-guns.'

They began laughing, then suddenly Jamie stopped. 'I can't stop thinking about Bob and that woman in the fur coat; just what was it with them? Bob helped us twice and the woman once, then you saw them together. That's just too big a co-incidence, don't you think?'

Todd shrugged. 'But where was they when Billy and his gang caught us?'

'That's true,' Jamie said thoughtfully. 'You do know, the longer we stay with the gang, the more chance we're going to get caught. And the punishment for being thieves in these days is really bad. We are only going to stay with them until we've got the money to see Catherine, aren't we?'

'Of course.' A smile slowly spread across Todd's face. 'I've just had a thought and it'll solve our money problems in one go.'

'What?'

Todd glanced briefly at Henry and the others and said, 'I'm going to get to that box Henry keeps the money in. I saw roughly where that boy got it from.'

'Have you gone mad?'

'They won't know; I'll creep round the outside in the shadows, then I'll fill my pockets.' He patted Jamie on the arm and said, 'Don't worry; you'll soon be looking through those telescopes on Hawaii.'

Jamie struggled for words. 'This... this is madness.'

Before Todd could answer, footsteps from the darkness drew their attention. It was Henry's mother. 'So what are you two talking about?' she asked, ambling towards them.

Todd's smile froze. 'Oh, nothing much, Mrs Holton.'

'Call me Mary,' she replied, smiling warmly. She spoke to Jamie. 'Your uncle must be worried, don't you fink?'

Jamie didn't reply; he was preoccupied by what he knew Todd was about to do.

Mary shook her head. 'You certainly don't belong 'ere. What is my son finking of?'

Just then a bell fixed to the wall rang three times, sounding the correct code.

Tension filled the air in an instant. Zad spoke with a West African dialect. 'If dat's J.T., somet'ing's wrong, he's way too early.'

Henry ordered Hawk to get the door.

The easy atmosphere of moments before vanished. A heavy silence fell; it was broken by a man's angry voice from beyond the room. 'They was everywhere, and there was more of 'em this time.'

Hawk returned with a tall, black-bearded man dressed in heavy, dark clothing, the rim of his hat shielded his eyes. With him was a young teenager who, like the man, was panting.

Henry jumped to his feet. 'What's 'appened, J.T.?'

'When we got to Wardour Street we was just about to do the blag when we was ambushed by the Peelers.' J.T. produced a large empty sack from under his coat and tossed it to the floor.

'The damn Peelers,' Henry cursed, slamming his hand down onto the desk.

'Where's Joe?' queried Zad.

J.T. shook his head ruefully. 'They got 'im. We was lucky to escape.'

Jamie shivered - this was just what he feared would happen to him and Todd. He turned to say that, but Todd wasn't there. Jamie scanned the room, just catching sight of him along the wall in the faint rays from the oil lamps. He was going for the moneybox!

Henry's hand slammed the desk again. 'Another good blagger gone.'

Philip sighed deeply. 'It's like they're closing in on us. First it was the posh gaffs, now they're pushing us back.'

'Like closing the net on the fish,' Swiper remarked.

Henry left the desk with a heavy sigh. 'Fings are getting worse, Zad,' he said.

'We can't even do the easy jobs now,' Swiper said in disgust, with pipe smoke billowing from his nostrils.

Jamie rubbed his hot forehead. He couldn't see Todd now. *What was he up to?*

'We'll just have to blag another gaff,' said Philip.

'I just don't like the way we're getting driven back,' Henry grumbled. He raised the rum bottle to his lips again. 'What else is there tonight?'

'That gaff at Soho Square,' Swiper said. 'I know on good aufority, it's still unattended.'

Henry nodded. His piercing blue eyes swung to Jamie, startling him. 'Where's Todd?' he growled.

Jamie tried to answer but nothing came from his lips. 'Where is he?' Henry demanded of the others.

Jamie froze.

'Todd!' Henry shouted, before snatching up an oil lamp and hurrying with some others of the gang, to the area where the strongbox was kept. Jamie closed his eyes and braced himself. He couldn't help Todd now! What would happen to them?

"E's here,' Billy announced, holding a lamp above where Todd lay by the side wall.

Jamie saw Todd yawn and rub his eyes. 'What's happened?' Todd said.

Henry squinted at Todd. After a tense pause, Henry announced, 'You're going to 'ave a taste of blagging with Jamie. Go wiv Swiper and Patch and do exactly what you're told. And Jamie, use your sling-shot if you 'ave to.'

Mary stepped out from the shadows. 'You can't use them, they're not experienced enough.'

'Well, this is 'ow they'll get experience, ain't it?' Henry retorted.

'I should run this place, I'd run it right,' Mary told him.

Henry's laugh was brief. 'I think Zad would 'ave somefing to say about that.'

Ignoring Mary and Zad glaring at each other, Henry ordered Swiper, 'Get going.'

'Swiper's the best, just do as 'e tells ya,' Billy assured them, then added, 'or you'll get caught.'

X

Jamie clutched the sacks he'd been given and Todd carried a crowbar.

Passing through the underground passageways, Todd whispered to Jamie, 'I couldn't find the box.'

'I can't believe what you tried to do,' said Jamie. It was impossible to see Todd in the dark.

'I want to find Hector too, you know!'

Jamie blindly patted Todd on the back. 'Glad to hear it.'

At 10 minutes past midnight, Jamie and Todd left the hideout. Patch had the collars of his heavy coat flicked up and had pulled on a black woolly hat to conceal his bright, white hair. Swiper had tied down the flaps of his deerstalker and put away his pipe; this was serious business.

Fog hovered throughout the city. Several times, they heard the sounds of revelry and realised that they must be passing a public house, but could not make it out in the swirling gloom. Shadowy images appeared and disappeared like phantoms of the underworld within the thick, stagnant mists, keeping Jamie on constant alert.

Swiper led the way through Soho Square, where the fog was so thick that only those trees bathed in the yellow smear of surrounding gaslights could be seen.

'Cor – I've never seen fog like this, it gives me the creeps, but it gives us a bit of cover,' said Todd.

'Shhh,' said Swiper. 'No talking.'

Todd walked in silence for a while but then said, 'Jamie, where's the church from here? In case something happens.'

'Don't ask *me!* You're the one with the sense of direction.'

Todd sidled up to Swiper. 'Where's St Giles High Street from here?' he whispered.

The thief frowned. 'Why?'

'We know someone there. If anything goes wrong, we can go to them.'

'Nuffin's going to go wrong.'

'Yeah, I know, but where is it, anyway?'

Swiper pointed. 'There's a road over there behind the fog. Go down it and go right then left, and you'll come to it.'

They scuttled across the road, to a dark-fronted house on the north side of the square.

Crouching by the front windows, his face half-illuminated by a street lamp close by, Swiper tied up the flaps on his deerstalker. 'Jamie, 'ave your sling-shot ready and if anyone comes let 'em 'ave it. Patch is going to be just behind the window; 'e'll let us know if the Peelers come.'

Swiper set to work on the downstairs window with the crowbar, and had it open it in seconds. He waved Todd, Jamie and Patch in first, then joined them inside.

'Just fill your sack with any metal objects you find,' Swiper said. 'Any china, wrap it in the rags I gave you. You're going to 'ave to use your sense of touch most of the time.'

Patch was left on lookout duty at the window. The others crept over the polished floorboards of a large room. The expert housebreaker got to work immediately. He searched a table with his fingertips and in no time at all had two candlesticks and a silver tea service in his sack.

Jamie's eyes began to adjust to the dark and he was soon able to pick out various objects, like two big leather armchairs and a sofa. Suddenly he spotted a large figure no more than 10 feet away! Why weren't they being apprehended by this giant of a man? Maybe he was waiting for them to get closer. 'Th – There's someone in the room with us,' Jamie whispered.

Swiper came to Jamie's side at once. 'Where?'

'There.'

Peering intently at a tall figure in the darkened room, Swiper sighed. 'It's a stuffed bear, muttonhead,' Swiper said irritably. 'Pull yourself togever. This room's done. Follow me.'

They moved to a big wood-panelled hallway, where windows by the front door let in some light from the street lamp outside.

By the stairs, Jamie again suddenly found himself face-to-face with a looming figure. He staggered back, gasping with fear - and then realised that it was just a suit of armour. 'Get a grip, Jamie,' he whispered to himself.

Swiper was inspecting a sword taken from the wall, when Jamie heard something on the stairs. He tiptoed over to Swiper. 'Didn't you hear that?'

''Ear what?'

'I heard the stairs creak.'

Swiper put the sword down. 'Houses creak all the time, but you never take notice of 'em during the day. Don't worry, this 'ouse is empty.'

Jamie watched the shadowy figure of Swiper picking up items, using his hands to detect their value.

'Youse two, check upstairs,' Swiper ordered in a low voice. 'I'll be wiv ya in a minute.' Jamie's heart sank. The sight of the stairs disappearing into darkness filled him with dread. 'Well, go on,' Swiper prompted.

Todd was first up. The higher they went the darker it became. Once Jamie reached the landing, he slumped against the wall, tightly gripping his sack.

'What's the matter?' Todd asked, walking back along the landing.

'I don't like this, Todd,' Jamie replied, between shallow breaths. 'I've just remembered the ghosts at my uncle's house.'

'Get a grip, Jamie, or we'll never make it home. Anyway, we're surrounded by ghosts, aren't we?'

Jamie gulped. 'What d'you mean?'

'We shouldn't be seeing all these people. In our time, they're all dead, aren't they?'

'Oh, great, I'm in a world filled with ghosts. That makes me fill a whole lot better.'

'Come on, Jamie, get moving.'

'I can't, I'm bricking it.' His head bumped against the wall as he took a deep breath. 'And this burglary lark is all right for you, you're used to breaking into places, I'm not!' Moments later, at the sound of Swiper climbing the stairs, his sack clinking with silverware, he breathed a sigh of relief. At least now he and Todd wouldn't be alone up here.

'Ain't you got anyfing yet?' asked Swiper, casting a disgusted look over them both.

'Sorry, Swiper,' said Todd. 'Jamie's scared.'

'I know. 'Ere, take this.' Swiper passed Todd the sack, which was almost full. 'Gimme yours.' Swiper opened a door. Jamie peered inside, but saw only blackness; again, fear rose in his throat. He swallowed hard and clenched his fists.

Swiper pointed. 'Try that room at the end. It should be pretty easy to see in there from the light outside.'

He was right; the rays from the street lamp did make it easier to see. Jamie moved across to a table and picked up a china figurine and wrapped it in a rag. He put it in the sack and picked up another and another, all the while gaining confidence.

Todd dropped a heavy ornament into the sack by the fireplace, making a loud clatter. 'Whoops!' he cried.

'Watch it clumsy,' warned Jamie, 'you'll get us... ' his voice faltered as one of the stairs creaked, followed by a scuffing sound. 'Did you hear that?'

'Yeah, all right, I didn't mean it.'

'No, I just heard something on the stairs.'

'But Swiper said houses creak all the time, didn't he? Don't worry.'

Jamie tried to swallow but his throat was dry. The darkness seemed to press itself against him. Get a grip, he told himself again. Do the job. And don't even think about ghosts... but then, he felt a presence - just as he had in Simon's back room. Beads of sweat broke out on his forehead. Raising one arm to wipe them away, he turned sharply, and found himself staring into a face as pale as death.

He cried out in terror and tried to run, but tripped over something and hit the floor. In panic, he scrambled across the floorboards to the fireplace, and crashed into Todd's legs.

'It's all right, it's Patch,' came Todd's calm voice.

Warily, Jamie got to his feet and shuffled to the centre of the room, where Patch stood. His face was so white that even now Jamie was still spooked by it.

Patch spoke for the first time in a slow voice, 'P-e-e-l-e-r-s.'

'What did he say?' Todd asked.

'P-e-e-l-e-r-s,' Patch repeated.

Swiper came into the room and glared at them. 'What's all the noise in 'ere? What is it, Patch?' He crossed to the window and looked out.

'The Peelers are outside,' Swiper said. 'Someone must 'ave seen us getting in here 'ere.'

'Oh, no, not the police!' Todd groaned, making for the door, his sack clanking.

Swiper moved swiftly from the window, and grabbed Todd's arm. 'You *can't* leave now.'

Todd stuttered, 'I-I don't want to be caught, we've got to get out of here.' Breaking free from Swiper's grip, he started to run, his sack banging against the walls as he scrambled along the dark landing.

Swiper chased after him.

An almighty noise made Jamie flinch; Todd had slipped at the top of stairs, letting go of the sack, which had spilled its contents down the stairs and onto the hallway.

'You idiot!' cursed Swiper.

After that, it was every boy for himself. Pushed roughly by Patch, Jamie hurried down the stairs. At the sound of footsteps on the path, he dived down, and braced himself, remaining still as a dark silhouette came up to the door and peered through the window. Jamie crawled into the front room where Patch was crouching by the window. A second figure appeared outside, just a couple of feet from where Patch was hiding. The broken window frame must have been spotted; the figure left the window to the sound of a long shrill blast of a whistle.

Patch pushed up the sash window and jumped out, ignoring an order to stop. Jamie ran to the window to escape but froze when he heard the clatter of running footsteps echoing in the square. A troop of lawmen carrying lighted lanterns came looming out of the fog. Jamie started to shake. What should he do? Where could he hide? With the sound of feet approaching, and seconds to spare, he dived behind the sofa.

Crouching there, he overheard an officer explaining that one had just got away. An order to pursue him rang out. At this, some turned and ran, but several others climbed through the window, their oil lamps illuminating the interior. Expecting to be discovered at any moment, Jamie could barely breathe as he watched the long shadows cast by the lamps dance on the ceiling. And then, the heavy charge rumbled away from the front room. He felt such a powerful rush of relief that, as he moved to get up, his legs almost gave way under him.

Acting on instinct, Jamie jumped over the sofa, shot out of the window, and set off at a sprint for the church in St Giles High Street. Without Todd there to guide him, he was relieved that he could remember Swiper's directions. There was no sign of any policemen, but he detected faint running footsteps behind him. A quick glance over his shoulder gave no indication of how close his pursuer was, and the shrouding mists concealed him.

If it was a policeman, why wasn't he blowing his whistle? Panic spurred Jamie on; the mystery pursuer's footsteps still audible in the quiet street.

Ahead, the white stone church in its grassy grounds emerged from the fog. Jamie raced through the gates and along the familiar gravel path, scrambled to the side of the church and squatted low to the ground.

All was quiet, apart from his own heavy breathing.

Where was his pursuer now?

He listened for footsteps but heard only silence. He peered around the corner of the church, trying to make out the path and the gateway but the blanket of fog, faintly lit by the gas lamps, revealed nothing.

He rested his head against the cold stonework.

Who *was* that chasing him? Was someone watching him now? And how was Todd faring? Had he managed to get away? Then it hit Jamie: *it was the ghosts from Simon's house who had been following them all along!*

Slow footsteps approached along the path. Then they stopped; silence once more. Jamie held his breath, bracing himself for coming face-to-face with the supernatural for the second time. He edged to the corner of the church, only to see drifting fog. Someone or something was definitely beyond the fog; the small stones on the path were being disturbed.

'Jamie!' Jamie jumped.

'Jamie,' it was Todd's voice. 'Where are you?'

Jamie let out a long sigh, and got to his feet.

'What's wrong?' Todd asked. 'You look petrified.'

'When I ran from the square, I was followed here.'

Todd scanned the area. 'Well... where are they now?'

Jamie sat back down against the church. 'Todd, it's the ghosts, I know it.'

Todd swallowed.

Jamie covered his face with his hands, and shook his head. He looked up at Todd with a frown. 'How did you escape?'

Todd sat down next to him. 'It was close. Just before the cops came charging into the hallway, I saw a handle on a small door in the wooden wall. I opened it and hid inside. When the cops went up stairs, I got out of there, quick.'

'I saw Patch escape, but I'm not sure if he got away. And what happened to Swiper?'

'I don't know.' Todd shook his head and said, 'I'm sorry I messed up, but you know how the police freak me out.'

Jamie hardly heard his friend's apology. He span round onto his knees in front of him, and said, 'Todd, I don't know why, but I think the ghosts I saw at my Uncle's house are following us in this time.'

Todd gulped. 'If it is *true,* why us?'

XI

The following morning, fine rain floated down from low, grey clouds. The heavy fog from the night before had lifted.

Jamie awoke under the church porch. He'd curled up his knees and he hugged his chest, to generate warmth - but still he was freezing cold as his eyes flickered open. The first thing he saw was a rat standing on its hind legs looking at him. It was no more than four feet away, and went scuttling off into the grass at Jamie's yelp. Then he noticed Todd's absence. Jumping up, he scanned the area and spotted him bending over by the railings being sick.

'You all right, Todd?' he called, crossing the wet grass.

Todd wiped his mouth with his sleeve and straightened up, holding his stomach. 'Not really. My stomach's been feeling really weird lately. I had the trots again, as well.'

'You must have the start of the flu or something.'

'I don't know what it is, but I hope they've got the medicine I need. *I'm so thirsty.*' He grimaced. 'I see your ghostly stalkers didn't strike last night.'

'No - but I'm not making it up, Todd,' Jamie replied, with a glance at the churchyard.

His eye was caught by a man on the other side of the church railings. He had a ladder resting against a lamp post and was putting out the flame. Jamie thought about his pursuer and wondered why he remained undetected. The man closed the glass front to the street lamp and moved away. Jamie glanced at the locked doors inside the porch. 'So what do we do? Wait for the vicar or rejoin the gang?'

'We don't need to do either,' Todd replied, rubbing his stomach.

'Why not?'

Todd reached into his sock and pulled out an emerald-encrusted gold necklace. 'I took this from the mantelpiece in that room when Patch told us about the cops outside.'

'Wow!' Jamie gasped at the necklace which sparkled as it dangled from Todd's hand.

'As I was feeling around the mantelpiece, my fingers touched this, and I thought, why should Henry have it when we could put it to better use?' Todd explained, with a grin. 'See, stealing isn't always bad, or shouldn't I've taken it?'

Jamie broke into a smile. 'Why didn't you tell me you had it?'

'I didn't want to, I was worried I had it on me all night, knowing how dangerous this time is.' He replaced the piece in his sock. 'Come on, let's find a jeweller's.'

***

Seven Dials was very different during the day. Most of the streets that met at the circular junction were packed with stalls, there were shoppers everywhere and horse-drawn carriages poured in from every direction, creating a big traffic jam.

Outside The Crown, two caped policemen maintained a horseback vigil, while two glaziers worked on the pub's broken window.

'I feel a lot safer here than I did the other night. The place seems quite civilised,' said Jamie, watching the glaziers at work – which reminded him of Bob beating up the three robbers, and breaking the window in the process.

He watched the hustle and bustle. What on earth would these 19th-Century Londoners make of the presence, in their midst, of two time-travellers from the future, he wondered.

He and Todd swerved to avoid the heaps of manure between the stationary traffic, as they crossed the junction and stopped outside a tailor's shop on the corner of a street. A big woman with a heavily stained, white apron leant against the door frame, with arms folded and a scowl on her face. An ugly wart on her chin and another above her eyebrow reminded Jamie of a witch in a book he'd read when he was little. The shop-front was almost entirely hidden by a variety of clothes fastened above the window, leaving only a narrow space as an entrance. A long table outside displayed smaller items and a few household goods.

'Who you gawping at?' she snapped. 'Be gone wiv ya, street brats!'

Jamie moved on to a second-hand furniture shop next door, which traded goods of the poorest quality. An elderly, gaunt, grey-bearded man stood outside. As they approached, he grinned, revealing a few crooked teeth. 'That's Mrs Strathmore,' he whispered. 'She hates strangers, especially kids.'

'That's a good way to run a business,' Todd remarked.

The shopkeeper chuckled.

'We're looking for a jeweller's. D'you know where there is one?' Jamie asked.

The old man stared at their threadbare clothing and said, in a low voice, 'Do you have... merchandise?' Jamie bit his lip and hesitated. 'It's all right, you can trust me. I know someone who's a bit... shall we say curved, instead of crooked, if you get my meaning? Jacob's a fair man, though.'

Jamie was about to reply when a group of youngsters came running along, kicking a bundle of rolled-up rags.

Todd laughed. 'I can't see myself practising with a ball of rags!'

The makeshift ball was kicked in their direction, giving Todd the chance to demonstrate his skills. He flicked the tightly wrapped bundle into the air and kept it clear of the ground by bouncing it on his right foot.

Jamie watched, impressed with Todd's ability, while the youngsters gathered, mesmerised. They'd probably never seen such footwork. Jamie chuckled when Todd even used his head to prevent the rags from landing on the road.

'If only you could do this, Jamie,' Todd said, 'you might've got yourself in the school team *and* the Riverside Posse.' At that moment he flinched and fell backwards, landing on a fresh pile of horse manure, much to the amusement of his young audience.

'Nice one, Todd!' Jamie said, looking down at him.

Todd clutched the back of his leg tightly, wincing with pain. 'I've got mental cramp,' he gasped. 'I've never had it this bad before.'

Jamie helped him up. 'You OK?'

Todd staggered on his good leg. 'Yeah, I'm all right, apart from the horse shit on my trousers. I've had enough of it, it's everywhere you look!'

Jamie laughed, then noticed Todd's gaunt features, which were highlighted by his heavy scowl.

The old man calling over his shoulder, interrupted Jamie's concern. 'Edward, your friends are here.'

From inside the shop, a young boy appeared.

The shopkeeper placed his hand on the boy's head. 'This is Edward, my grandson. I'll show you that jeweller's.' The old fellow waved his hand. 'Follow me. Edward, mind the shop, till I get back.'

**

A few minutes later, Jamie pushed open the door to a small jeweller's shop not far from Seven Dials, and stepped onto a wooden floor. He found himself surrounded by trinkets of every description; one side of the shop was entirely filled with clocks, which ticked in unison.

Two men sat behind the counter. One of them, much older than the other, and wearing a red waistcoat and black bow tie, was peering through a magnifying eyeglass at a gold chain. The other greeted the boys.

Todd went up to the counter and showed them the necklace. 'We need two sovereigns for this, Mister.'

Jamie sighed. Why had Todd told them how much they wanted? The necklace could be worth a lot more.

'Let me see,' said the older jeweller, holding out his hand.

Once he set eyes on the necklace, he put down the chain he was holding. 'Where did you acquire such a necklace?' he asked, reaching for it.

'It's my grandmother's. She asked me to sell it for her,' Todd told him confidently.

The jeweller glanced briefly at his assistant, then bent his head to study the gems through the eyeglass. 'Hmm... hmm.' He removed the eyeglass and turned to the young man. 'Fetch two sovereigns, will you?'

'Wait a minute,' Jamie interjected. 'I know my friend said we wanted two sovereigns, but I think it could be worth a lot more than that.'

The jeweller sneered. 'You say it belongs to your grandmother?' Todd nodded. 'Poppycock and you know it. The only way this could possibly have come into your possession is if you stole it. And you did, didn't you? I've got a good mind to fetch the police.'

'All right, all right,' Jamie had no choice but to yield.

The young man returned from the back of the shop and handed the money over.

Jamie glimpsed at the two gold shiny coins in Todd's hand. At last, they had the money to see Catherine.

Once outside the shop, Jamie said bitterly, 'When you're selling something, Todd, you don't say how much you want before they've even looked at it! We're lucky we've already got enough change for a cab.'

Todd seemed absentminded. He nodded vaguely. 'I need to get to a toilet, quick,' he said, looking around for one.

***

'You two again!' The uniformed man at the Science Institute rose from his desk. He raised his eyebrows at the gleaming coins in Todd's dirt-encrusted palm.

'You said you'd let us see Catherine,' Jamie said.

'Miss Wallace to you, my lad.' The man pocketed the sovereigns. 'What happened to you? I thought you said your parents were rich.'

'We've had a run of bad luck.' Jamie was already tired of the small talk.

'It can't be that bad if you have a pocket full of sovereigns,' the man laughed. 'She's giving a lecture at the moment. She'll be finished soon, but I'll get you into the auditorium.'

Jamie felt a thrill of excitement; he was about to meet the famed astronomer, the scientist Simon had told him about. He knew how much his uncle would have loved to be in his position.

The man took them along an elegant corridor with deep polished floorboards. Crystal chandeliers hung from the ceiling which was edged with fine moulded cornices.

Very quietly, he opened double doors onto a view of packed rows of curved seats. 'Stand here and when she's finished, go and see her. And *don't* tell her I let you in.'

But Jamie had no further interest in the man. His eyes fell upon the slender woman on the stage, no more than 60 feet away. With her high cheekbones and full red lips, she was beautiful. She spoke with a Scottish accent, addressing her audience of young students and scientists. A model of the solar system, supported on a large bench, stood next to her. The planets were suspended by wire around the sun. Next to the model stood a big clock-face, fixed above a complexity of brass cogs.

'So as I mentioned earlier,' Catherine was saying, 'Sir Isaac Newton made some great discoveries. He investigated the forces of nature in a quantitive way. By his theory of gravitation, he showed how simple mathematical laws regulated the universe. If Sir Isaac had never taken up science, we wouldn't be where we are now with *our* discoveries.' She moved to one side and pointed at the model. 'The solar system is a gargantuan clock in its own way, the planets are the cogs and the Sun is what powers these heavenly cogs, just as the pendulum does on a clock. I just hope the Sun doesn't stop, as all pendulums ultimately do.' A ripple of laughter passed through the audience. 'So there you are, gravity is a simple but very powerful force; it governs everything, from fleas to the mighty oceans. Thank you.' Enthusiastic applause followed, with Jamie eagerly joining in. 'Any questions?'

A young man stood up. 'Could gravity be used as a means to power trains and ships, some time in the future?' he asked.

'Good heavens,' she said with a smile. 'I think you're in the realms of fantasy, there.' Laughter followed her remark. 'Being serious for a moment, I think your question is quite interesting though… but no, gravity comes from the earth itself, and the moon to a certain extent. Though there are some far-out theories that say a space vessel could use gravitational pulls to propel it, once it reached space - but they're just pure speculation. Any more questions? Yes, you.'

Another young man was standing. 'Talking of the moon, what is known of its dark side?'

'In a word, nothing. There are certain hypotheses, but we just don't know.'

'Where's Hector Lightfoot?' called someone in the audience.

She smiled ruefully. 'As I've said many times before, I have no knowledge of Hector's whereabouts.'

Todd gave Jamie a nudge.

'Why did he disappear the way he did?'

Catherine shrugged. 'Only Hector knows that.'

'It's been rumoured he was working on a secret project... and as you worked with him, you *must* know more than you're telling,' the questioner persisted.

She sighed. 'That's it, I must go. Thank you.'

She left, through a door beside the stage, to a round of applause. Students began to drift away from the auditorium.

Jamie knocked on the door Catherine had used and entered the annexed study. There was no sign of the astronomer, but he was immediately drawn to the array of brass instruments set out on tables. Then a big brass telescope fixed to a tripod close to the windows caught his eye, and he walked over to it and twiddled with the lens.

Another door to the study opened and Catherine appeared. 'Who on earth are you?' she demanded sharply.

Jamie stepped forward. 'We're here to see you about something really important.'

'Really? What is it?'

Jamie hesitated, looking across to Todd.

'Well?'

After another glance at Todd, Jamie answered, 'We're from the future, Miss; we were sent back in time and have been here since... '

'This is a joke, isn't it?'

'No, Miss, honest. We need to see Hector Lightfoot, so he can help us get back to the 21st Century.'

'Leave my study at once!' she ordered. 'And you can tell Cornelius, I do *not* know where Hector is.'

'Who's Cornelius?' Jamie asked. 'We don't know anyone of that name.'

Catherine marched over to the door, her long dress rustling. 'I want to be left alone to get on with my work.'

Todd frowned. 'We're telling the truth, Miss,' he said.

'Prove what you tell me. Show me something wondrous from the future.' Jamie exchanged a look with Todd. 'Just as I thought.'

'We could've showed you our mobile phones if we had them on us,' said Todd, with a despondent shrug.

'Your *what?*'

Jamie knew this was probably their one and only chance to convince her. 'Miss Wallace, please don't throw us out. Just listen to what we have to say, that's all I ask.'

Catherine sucked on her cheek. 'Very well.'

Jamie began. 'We've been sent back in time by Hector's time-travelling device, and we need his help, desperately.' He ignored Catherine's scowl, and her hand on the doorknob. 'And we haven't been sent by someone to find Hector's whereabouts.'

'This won't work, you know, and you can tell Cornelius that.'

Jamie and Todd answered together. 'We don't know Cornelius!'

Catherine's scowl remained. 'If you're from the future, why are you dressed in these rags, and why have you got a black eye?'

'We was robbed of our clothes,' Todd explained. 'And I got punched in the face. I also had a fight with another boy.'

'*Prove* to me that you are from the future.'

Todd shook his head. 'We have nothing on us from the future.'

'Man lands on the moon in 1969,' Jamie announced. 'A giant telescope is sent into orbit in our time, called the Hubble Telescope. It's named after an astronomer. And your model on the stage is inaccurate; there are nine planets, not eight. In 1930, Pluto is discovered.' He hesitated. 'Although it was voted a dwarf planet by the world's astronomers, so I suppose there *are* only eight planets.'

'I'm not convinced by all this. How can it be proved? Catherine Wallace walked over to her desk and leant against it. She laughed briefly. 'Time-travel is not possible, so why do you come to me making these absurd claims?'

'Because you helped Hector on that iron arch under the British Museum, which *is* a time-travelling device and you know where he's hiding,' Jamie said. He could not afford to back down.

Catherine shook her head. 'Cornelius is behind this ruse. I'm sure of it. How did you get in?'

'We sneaked in,' Todd replied.

'Right, that's it.' She marched over to the door and snatched it open. 'I want these two boys removed!' she called into the auditorium, her reddened cheeks contrasting dramatically with her white, frilly tunic.

'You're making a big mistake,' Todd told her. 'We're stranded here.'

A man came to the study.

'Escort these two from the premises, Gordon, and tell Alfred at the front desk to watch out for them, not to let them back in.'

'Right you are, Miss Wallace. Come with me.' The man grabbed Jamie around the waist.

Jamie gasped at the man's strength. 'Wait!' he yelled, but Gordon wasn't having any of it; he began dragging Jamie from the room. 'I can prove it!' he bleated. 'There's two astronomers... Miller and, er, Huggins.' Catherine appeared from the annexe on hearing the two names. She listened, arms folded. 'Next year, in 1863, they're going to bring out a telescope installed with photographic apparatus. I know this, because I read it in a book... in the 21st Century.'

'Gordon, wait!'

Gordon snorted. 'Shall I take him to Bedlam, Miss Wallace?'

'No!' The astronomer laughed briefly. 'Let him go, I want to talk with him again.'

'Are you sure?'

'Yes, but please wait around, just in case.'

She waited until Gordon closed the door and left. 'That is not common knowledge. How could you possibly know that? I spoke with them only the other day and they told me that I am one of a selected few who knows about their photographic telescope.'

'Please believe me, I *did* read that in the 21st Century, in one of my astronomy books.'

After a lengthy pause she said, 'Tell me how you got here.'

'My uncle was showing us around the laboratory, and whilst we were in there alone, lightning struck the building, there was a bright light and here we are.'

'Lightning?' she said, almost to herself.

Jamie sensed her resolve melting.

But then it surged back, stronger than before. 'No,' she said. 'What am I thinking of? Cornelius's scientists probably know the two astronomers, and as for the lightning theory, well, they made it up.' She opened the door.

Jamie slammed the door shut. 'I *can* prove we're from the future.' He knew he had only seconds to convince her, or she'd be calling for Gordon again. He turned to Todd and asked, 'D'you remember that experiment we did at school, when we created an electric current from lemons?'

Todd looked blank. 'I didn't bother with it,' he said. 'You know I hate science.'

'You hate every lesson,' Jamie muttered. He addressed Catherine once more. 'If I can create an electric current from lemons, will that convince you?'

'You are claiming you can produce electricity from *lemons*?'

'It will be a weak current, but yes, I can. At least give me a chance. What have you got to lose?'

'Very well. I'm only intrigued about these lemons, but I have no knowledge of Hector's whereabouts.'

Jamie settled for that. Now he had to remember the apparatus. 'I need four lemons, four strips of copper... erm... four strips of zinc, they're the electrodes. And five wires with clips attached.'

Catherine opened the door again. 'I'll get Gordon to fetch the things you need,' she said, shaking her head.

***

Jamie and Todd's stay of execution went on for almost two hours whilst Gordon accumulated the items on Jamie's list. When he finally returned with the equipment, he wanted to stay and see what conclusion could be made with such strange items, but Catherine sent him away and locked the door.

Jamie placed the four lemons on one of the benches and pushed a zinc and a copper strip into each one. He thought hard to remember the test as he went along; failure would get them thrown out. Meticulously, he connected an end of one wire to a zinc strip and the other end to a copper strip fixed to a different lemon. He did this to all of them, creating a circuit. One connection to a copper strip was left free, as was a zinc strip.

This done, Jamie glanced at Catherine. She stood silent but watchful.

'Todd, pull the curtains,' said Jamie.

Within moments the room was dark.

Jamie took a wire in each hand. 'I have a negative and a positive,' he said. When he heard Todd return to the bench, he touched the two ends together, creating a minute spark. Tapping the ends to emphasise the electric current, he said, 'Now do you believe us? The electricity comes from the acid in the lemons. This is a *20th-Century* discovery. Open the curtains, Todd.'

Daylight filled the room. Since Catherine was expressionless, Jamie couldn't tell what she thought of his display. Was she convinced?

'Oh, my word,' she whispered. 'Electricity from lemons, it's incredible!' She laughed briefly. 'I would so much like to show that to Faraday, but I can't tamper with history. I can't show *anyone!*'

'So you believe us, then?' Todd asked.

'Yes,' she said faintly and smiled at them. She studied their threadbare clothing and Todd's bruised eye. 'You poor lambs. What must you be going through?'

'So where *is* Hector?' Todd asked.

Catherine walked to one of the windows. Looking up at the grey sky, she said, 'My dear boys, it doesn't matter where Hector is, for there is no way back to your time.'

Jamie touched her arm. 'There *must* be a way to our time; we got here, didn't we? So we can go back.' He knew he must sound frantic.

'That arch is a mechanism for time-travel, but it is not possible.' She looked upset.

'Why not?' Todd asked. He, too, sounded desperate.

'The museum is heavily guarded, Cornelius suspects Hector might return to use the arch.'

Jamie nodded. 'There were men guarding the lab when we arrived. They almost caught us.'

'What I'm about to do is forbidden. Hector's life is in danger. But tonight I'll take you to him; he can explain. Now I have some things to do; you must stay here.' She put on a long coat, preparing to leave. 'I'll be back as soon as I can. Sorry, I must lock you in for your own safety.'

As the key turned in the lock, Todd smiled. 'Well done again, Jamie. You've saved the day.'

Jamie wandered among the benches, his curiosity aroused by one of the instruments with many brass springs and cogs. 'Doesn't matter now, though, does it?' he said. 'We're going to see Hector at last, but we can't go home.' He stopped at another brass apparatus. 'And talking about home and our past... or should I say future? Whatever it is, doesn't exist, so we mustn't think of home any more.'

XII

The boys had been waiting for Catherine for hours.

'Where is she?' a worried Jamie demanded. He was standing by the window and peering out. 'Something's happened, she's been ages.'

Todd didn't answer; he sat in a chair holding his stomach. Over the proceeding hours, his abdominal pain had steadily worsened.

Looking yet again out of the window, Jamie said, 'What if she doesn't come back tonight, then what?'

Just then a key turned, accompanied by the sound of Catherine's reassuring Scottish brogue. 'I'm so sorry I didn't come back earlier, I got delayed by a pressing engagement. Here, I have some bread and cheese; it's all I could get.'

Todd attempted to stand up but remained bent over.

'What's wrong with you?' Catherine asked.

Todd winced. 'My stomach hurts. I need water.'

'You can have water soon.'

Jamie almost snatched the food from Catherine and tore at the loaf ravenously but Todd couldn't eat.

'Oh my, you must be very hungry,' Catherine said.

Jamie nodded, his mouth full of bread and cheese.

'I have a cab waiting. Follow me.'

Jamie walked with Todd and Catherine down the darkened corridor. In the foyer was the silhouette of Alfred, the man of the front desk. He was illuminated by a gas lamp in the porch as he stood by the doors. He approached them, fretting. 'I still don't understand what all this is about, Miss Wallace, sneaking out in such a clandestine manner.'

'Don't worry, Alfred, and please don't tell anyone about this.'

'Of course not, Miss Wallace.' He held open the doors and bade them goodnight.

The scraping of a hoof on the cobbles drew Jamie's attention in the gloom, he could just make out a hansom cab parked a short way from the entrance.

'What time is it?' he asked, stuffing another chunk of bread in his mouth.

'It's just after 10,' Catherine replied, before instructing the driver, 'Now, on to the last destination.'

'So where is Hector hiding out?' Jamie asked.

'Excuse me if I don't tell you. Hector's whereabouts must remain secret. But I can tell you that a dear friend of his, who happens to be a Lord, has given him indefinite loan of a property he owns. He arranges secret deliveries of food too, so Hector is well looked after.'

The cab left the grounds of the Science Institute with its two lanterns shining ahead like beams from a lighthouse.

'Now then,' Catherine said. 'Hector does not know you are coming. I haven't seen him for months.'

'Why is he hiding? Who's after him?' Jamie demanded.

There was a long silence; only the sound of the horse's hooves echoed in the street. 'Some... very dark forces,' she finally said. 'His life is in grave danger.'

'But what is it that this Cornelius wants?'

'It's better that I don't say.'

After travelling a short distance, the cab turned sharply, prompting Catherine to turn and look ahead. 'We're approaching the river. Not far now.'

The cab rumbled along the deserted street towards London Bridge, where the fog hung even more thickly, hovering above the Thames, engulfing the cab. A horn sounded eerily somewhere in the distance as they crossed the river.

'What's that?' Jamie asked, unnerved.

'A ship's horn, warning other vessels.'

They travelled a further couple of miles or so into the south of London. The road was dark and full of potholes. Big, detached houses were barely visible in the fog. Here, there was no street lighting. Catherine counted the houses then called for the driver to stop. She settled the fare and their cab departed slowly, rocking over the uneven road surface.

The sound of the wheels died away. 'Follow me,' Catherine whispered. 'Don't make a sound.'

She led them towards a large, three-storey town house.

'It's deserted,' said Jamie.

'Shhh,' Catherine warned.

Jamie concentrated on following the path through an unkempt garden. Beside the house, he could just make out a driveway, shut off by tall, wooden gates fixed with sharp metal spikes.

Not a word was spoken whilst Catherine put a key into the front door. Uneasily, Jamie entered an ocean of blackness, taking small shuffling footsteps until Catherine closed the door quietly. As the lock clunked shut, a loud scream rang out and the three of them cowered in terror.

Jamie had taken only a few steps when he felt something heavy ensnaring them. Then a sudden burst of light exploded, hurting his eyes.

'Who are you? State your identity, or I swear I'll run you through!' a voice roared.

Jamie peered through the netting which now covered them, and saw a man holding a lantern that burned a brilliant white light in one hand, and a gleaming rapier in the other.

'Hector, it's Catherine!'

'Soaring eagles!' the man cried. 'What on earth are you doing here?' He placed the lantern on the floor and freed them from the netting.

'That's not the best welcome I've ever had, I must say,' said Catherine regaining her composure.

'Terribly sorry, Catherine dear, I thought you were intruders.'

Jamie stole a glance at the man; he wore a dark, swallow-tailed coat and matching trousers. His hair was greying and grew past his collar. The two-inch scar on his right cheek was exactly as in the painting on Colonel Ramsbottom's wall and a wild light gleamed in his eyes.

The light inside the lantern began to flicker, then it burst into flames. The man stamped on it frantically and once again they were shrouded in blackness.

'Blast. The magnesium's expired far too soon.' Hector struck a match and lit a gas wall-lamp. Moments later, he lit a second lamp, and they saw a large table and six chairs, in a finely decorated room.

Catherine observed the smoking lantern sceptically. 'It was quite effective... whilst it lasted.'

'Oh, it's one of my defensive devices; just something I put together.'

Catherine smiled and walked towards him. 'You look so different with your long hair.'

They met in the middle of the room and held hands. 'Well,' Hector told her, 'being practically imprisoned in this house somewhat prevents me going to the barber-shop, though I always keep myself clean-shaven.' He froze then whispered, 'Are you sure you weren't followed here?'

Catherine shook her head. 'No, we weren't. I'm sure of it. I didn't hear any pursuing vehicles.'

'Hmm, they have been known to silence their horses' hooves and the wheels on their carriages, you know.' Slowly, Hector turned to Jamie and Todd. 'And who on earth are these two?'

'These two… are the future.'

'I beg your pardon?'

'Jamie, Todd, this is Hector Lightfoot. Hector, may I present Jamie and Todd. They are from the 21st Century.' Hector's mouth opened slowly. 'And they've had a tumultuous time since arriving, having been in fights and had their clothes stolen.'

Hector spoke softly. 'Soaring eagles.' Inspecting them as if looking at some rare exhibit for the first time, he said, 'This can't be possible, Catherine.' He broke into a broad grin and repeated his statement.

'I know, it's incredible.' Catherine told him how the lightning bolt had triggered the mechanisms in the arch. 'And my theory,' she added, 'is that the lightning absorbed the energy rays and carried them to the arch.'

Hector was hardly listening. All of a sudden, he asked, 'Do they have flying machines in your time?'

'Yes,' replied Todd.

Hector nodded thoughtfully. 'And what about space-travel, have they ventured out?'

This was Jamie's moment. He told Hector about the moon landings and the space probes sent to planets in the solar system and beyond. Eventually, Catherine intervened. 'Enough of this, Hector. There are more pressing matters to discuss.' She rested her hands on Jamie's and Todd's shoulders and said, solemnly, 'I have told these two that there's no way back to their own time.'

Hector went to the fireplace and struck a match. It took a while to get the coals burning. After checking that the curtains were firmly closed he looked at a watch on a chain from his waistcoat and waved everyone to the table, where he rested the sword. 'There's always hope,' he said.

Todd sat on something and jumped up, arching his back with a questioning look. He reached down and then held up some coiled rubber tubing with metal fixings on both ends and a thick folder.

'Ah, I'll take those,' said Hector.

Jamie managed to read *Discovering Diseases,* written in bold black lettering on the front of the folder, before Hector shoved it under the table.

'This is another defence mechanism,' said Hector, holding the tubing aloft. 'It fixes to a water main over there, which I've diverted from the kitchen.' He frowned at Todd. 'What's the matter with you?'

'I've got cramp in my back,' said Todd, rubbing his spine. 'And I need water.'

Catherine apologised for forgetting Todd's thirst, and left for the kitchen.

'Hmm,' said Hector, thoughtfully. 'Have you suffered any other cramp recently?'

'I got bad cramp earlier, in my leg, and I've had bad pains in my stomach.'

'And what about sickness and diarrhoea?'

Todd nodded. 'What have I got, Hector? Is it the flu?'

Catherine returned with a glass of water. She handed it to Todd and frowned. 'Hector, a few moments ago, you said there's always hope. What are you implying? Have you the means for time-travel?'

'I just said there's always hope,' Hector said, raising his hands, quelling any excitement. He pointed at Jamie and Todd. 'This is just fascinating, Catherine, and terribly exciting. He rubbed his hands together, and grinned at the boys. Then, turning to Catherine again, he asked, 'How could it have possibly happened without the use of the crystal?'

'It must have been such a terrific electric charge, taking the place of the crystal. It triggered the time mechanisms,' she suggested.

Jamie told them how he and Todd suffered a lot of pain when they were sent back in time.

'Really?' Jamie found it hard to read Hector's expression. 'That must have happened because of the absent crystal.'

'I agree,' said Catherine thoughtfully.

'So how does the time-travelling device work?' Jamie asked.

Hector smiled. 'What a question!' He scratched his head. 'I'll try to keep it simple, but stop me if I get too deep. The arched time-device can only be used when the moon is visible in the sky, night or day, whether there is cloud cover or not. The moon is used as a reflector; a reflector of rays of energy from the stars.'

'Wait a minute,' said Jamie.' I think the energy from the stars sounds like what are known as cosmic rays in our time.'

'Is that so?' said Hector, brow raised. 'Cosmic rays,' he muttered. 'Sounds fascinating.' He looked at Catherine. 'I think your theory regarding the lightning absorbing the *cosmic rays* is correct. I would say the moon was on show when the lightning struck and somehow transferred the rays directly to the arch. You see, these energy rays that come from the stars are from the beginning of time. The rays are in constant movement in the heavens. The moon reflects this energy with the aid of light energy that comes from the sun. A concentration of rays is then gathered by the magnetic arch, which acts as a relay... Are you following me?'

Jamie nodded eagerly, but Todd looked perplexed.

The engineer went on. 'Where was I? Ah, yes, so when the cosmic rays enter the magnetic arch, the crystal filters the rays, selecting matter for the correct time frame. And gravity is used to hold, or you could say suspend, the time-traveller out of time until the crystal filters one to the desired time. The process actually takes a while, but due to your suspension in time it feels a lot quicker! So there you have it, in layman's terms, of course.'

'Wow!' Jamie cried. 'That's amazing!' He turned to Todd and was amused to see that his friend looked baffled.

'But we had our problems constructing it, didn't we, Catherine?' continued Hector. 'Our work began to show signs of fruition about two years ago. I couldn't believe we were on the threshold of time-travel. Then came the day which really excited us. It was October last year, when I sent a canary a month into the future. A living thing sent through time. Wasn't it a fantastic occasion, Catherine?' She nodded, solemn-faced. 'Destiny was calling. We set the time machine in late November last year. The date was set one year into the future; December 1st. The same date you two arrived, I presume?'

Todd nodded. 'That's right; I remember reading that date on a newspaper, the day we arrived.'

'We wanted to test it but I never got the chance,' Hector said, dolefully.

'Tell them about Cornelius.'

'Yes, our Dutch friend, Cornelius Van Huls. Initially, I thought he was an honourable man working for the same great cause; but he is a ruthless man, who leads an undercover organisation called The Secret Operations Bureau, made up of both British and Dutch. It's so secret that neither our Parliament or the Prime Minister knows anything about it. Cornelius will stop at nothing to achieve his aim. I thwarted his dastardly plot, which he calls The Grand Plan, by taking a vital component. And that's when I went into hiding.'

'What does he want time-travel for?' asked Jamie.

'It's too preposterous for words, but I can tell you this: if he achieves his aim, it would harm the world in an immeasurable way.'

'Jamie's uncle told us about your expedition to China, Hector,' said Todd. 'What happened there?'

'My, you are well-informed,' said Hector. He gazed into the blackness, his face partly illuminated by the flames. 'A few years ago, I had the honour of working with Brunel. It was somewhat enjoyable.' He chuckled. 'I have fond memories of my time with him. A great man and sadly missed. 'Anyway, it seems there was something lacking within me. After working in America on locomotives, which made me quite wealthy and achieved much recognition, I realised I wanted something special in my life. I was good friends with Catherine's father and asked his permission for his daughter's hand in marriage. He readily agreed - but she readily refused.'

Catherine looked coyly at her hands and an awkward silence followed. Then she said, 'I was a young woman. You're 20 years older. And it wouldn't have worked anyway. Our beliefs would have clashed.'

Hector smiled fondly at her, 'I suppose you're right, my dear.' He sighed. 'I miss your father terribly, he was a great scientist and would have been very proud of your success in astronomy.' Hector looked at Jamie and Todd with a sad smile. 'He died of cholera 10 years ago. After Catherine refused to marry me, I needed something to do. Do you know that I served in the army?'

Todd grinned. 'Yeah, sounds really mental.'

'Mental?'

'Oh, we say that when something's unbelievable.'

'Oh, I see.' Hector was briefly bemused, but soon returned to his reminiscences with a smile. 'I could tell you boys some stories!'

'Tell us one,' Todd urged.

'I was part of an invasion force that attacked the coastal town of Aden, in the Middle East. British shipping was threatened, so we were sent in. I was there when the bombardment began, and one of the first to storm the beaches. After taking the town, I helped to build a coaling station for British steamships, going to and from India. Soon after, however, I was sent to Afghanistan.'

'Did you get that scar in battle?' Todd asked, after finishing his water.

Hector smiled awkwardly causing the scar to bend on his cheek. 'A battle of sorts, I suppose. Let's just say it involved a scorned woman and a chamber pot.'

Catherine laughed.

'How is your stomach, Todd?' Hector asked. 'Has the water helped?'

Todd nodded. 'Yes, the pain seems to have gone.'

'Good.'

'We met your army friend, Colonel Ramsbottom,' said Jamie.

Hector raised his eyebrows. *'You've met Godfrey?'* He lowered his voice, 'How was he?'

Jamie hesitated. 'His mind's gone. He talks to a painting of you on the wall.'

Hector closed his eyes. 'Poor Godfrey. I heard about his affliction just before I went into hiding. He saved my life, you know, during the Afghan campaign. An exceedingly brave man.'

'I know about the Afghan campaign,' said Jamie. 'You were on a hill, defending the artillery gun, when you were shot in the back. I've read some of the Colonel's journal.'

'Really?' Hector asked. 'Good for you! So, to continue, there I was, working on developing steam trains, which reminds me; since hiding here, I've made a steam contraption, it's just something I put together. I call it the steam carriage express; I must test it sometime.

'Hector! You are digressing again,' Catherine chided.

'So I am. Where was I?'

'China?' Catherine hinted.

'Oh, yes, China - I was invited to go there at the beginning of '52 to explore a mysterious mountain range called Oilian Shan. A British general in charge of a small unit during the first Opium War had come across a secret tribe there. He returned to England with some strange stories about these people. I, and only five others on the expedition, were told that his unit was attacked by the tribe. The general reported wounding a number of them, some seriously. Well, the following day the tribe's wounded men returned for battle, but their wounds were no more; the injuries inflicted on them, just 24 hours previously, had completely healed.'

'What?' Todd exclaimed. 'How could that be?'

The engineer smiled. 'You may well be confused, young Todd. The general certainly was. He ordered a retreat. Neither he nor his men could believe what they had witnessed.'

'You've never told me this, Hector,' said Catherine. 'Are you saying that the tribe had travelled forward through time to engage in battle, and then went back until their wounds had healed?'

Hector nodded. 'They must have, and the only explanation was that they had the means for time-travel. So we set off to make contact with them. The mountains proved hard going, so we split up into small groups of six. I lost contact with the rest of my group during a blizzard one night - it blew our tent down a ravine. I stumbled across a small crevice in the rocks and stayed there huddled under the blanket from my pack. At dawn, I awoke with a strange feeling. The blizzard had blown itself out, and everything was totally silent. When I stood up, there was still no sign of my group, but I was confronted by the strangest sight. At first, I thought I was looking at creatures with black fur and antlers, standing on their hind legs. I realised they were humans wearing bearskins, their faces hidden by black masks. They then advanced towards me, waving weapons that looked like cudgels.'

'So what did you do?' asked Jamie.

'I quickly retrieved my sword,' Hector picked up the weapon from the table and stood up, thrusting it, 'and charged at them! But not for long, I was covered in netting.'

'That's how *you* welcomed *us,* Hector,' Catherine reminded him, with a smile.

'Yes, indeed.' Hector laughed. 'Quite effective, isn't it?'

'Mmm,' she agreed.

'Go on, Hector!' urged Todd. 'What happened next?'

'I was taken prisoner, and kept in underground caves. During my incarceration, the High Priest's 12-year-old son became seriously ill with a raging fever. I managed to persuade them to let me attend to him, using the medicine in my kit. And I saved him from certain death.'

'Wow! So they set you free?' Jamie enquired.

'It was better than that; the High Priest pardoned me and they let me join the Xuni tribe. Eventually, I learned their complex language and even got a seat on the ruling council.'

'Wicked! cried Todd.

Jamie nodded, and asked, 'But why didn't they just travel to the future and find a cure for the priest's son, Hector?'.

'I was coming to that. The episode involving the wounded men was led by a rogue priest, who was jaunting through time with a few of the tribe, causing all kinds of mayhem. When the High Priest learnt about their exploits, it was decided that the time device was never to be used again.'

'Hear, hear,' agreed Catherine.

'Oh, come on, Catherine. What *I* wanted to do with it should be applauded.'

'I have always said that I don't approve of time-travel; as an astronomer, I think that the laws of physics should be left alone; the future does not belong to us.'

'So why did you assist me?' Hector asked.

'Because I allowed you to persuade me, which was obviously a mistake! I always said it would result in disaster and it has. Apart from the fiendish plot, look at the travesty regarding these boys. It's cursed I tell you, cursed.'

Hector shrugged. 'Maybe. So - there I was, aware they had a time-travel device, but I couldn't get to it. After spending three years with them, the day came that was to be the most amazing day of my life. The High Priest's son, Yugi, who had become a close friend, revealed to me their *Mun Vantzu Pex:* Portal To Tomorrow. I set out to ascertain exactly how the time-travelling device worked and somehow get back to England. It was hard leaving Yugi, but one night I packed all the scientific scrolls and took the one vital component, and left. Dishevelled and suffering from malnutrition, I eventually reached a British diplomat in Shanghai and asked for passage on a ship back to England. Immediately upon my return, I went to the Science Council, insisting that I be allowed to work on the project. They agreed and gave me an assignment at once.'

'What if Cornelius finds you here?' asked Jamie.

'I have constructed some fiendish defence mechanisms.' He beamed mischievously at Catherine who, obscurely, smiled back at him and rolled her eyes. 'Outside, I have rigging packed above the windows, ready to be discharged. I just need to pull down a lever over there. It will cover a large area, so is enough to immobilise an armed unit. It's something I put together when I first moved here; and I have my emergency case, too, filled with other defence devices.'

'Cool,' said Todd, 'I'm impressed.'

Hector was too intent on his account to query the strange use of the word 'cool'. 'It's time to reveal something to you,' he said. 'Come with me.' He led them down a dark, narrow passageway, their footsteps ringing out on its bare floorboards. The room they entered next was like a laboratory, and was lit by wall-lamps. Several tables held lengths of copper piping and a variety of many metal objects.

'Just look at all this!' said Jamie, letting out a long, low whistle at the array of glass jars, and test-tubes in racks, and a big microscope, which was surrounded by stacks of paper. As he reached out towards one of the jars, Hector's voice boomed. 'Come away from there, at once!'

Jamie's arm dropped, and he turned to see the engineer stomping towards him. In the time it took to cross the room, however, Hector had calmed down. 'That is of no concern to you,' he said, putting an arm around Jamie's shoulder and leading him away from the bench.

'That was rather uncalled for Hector,' said Catherine, with a disapproving look.

Hector smiled wryly. 'It's an experiment I'm working on, and it's at a delicate stage.'

Catherine's attention turned to two tilting tables in the room. 'These drawings look familiar, Hector,' she said, studying diagrams fixed to them. Then it dawned on her. 'You *have* constructed a time-travelling device, haven't you?'

Hector smiled broadly and his eyes gleamed.

Jamie looked for an iron arch, but there wasn't one.

Hector removed a blanket from a grandfather clock, which stood slightly taller than him. 'And here it is,' he said, with a showman-like gesture. 'My time machine.'

Catherine approached the clock slowly. 'I... don't understand,' she said, with a puzzled frown on her face.

'What? That I've built a time machine inside a grandfather clock? I'm not spoilt for choice confined to this house, you know, though I am fortunate Lord Appleby dabbles in science, so all the materials I needed, he provided. There was quite a lot at my disposal, but a clock is very apt, wouldn't you say?'

Catherine stroked the walnut case, staring at the small varnished door to the trunk. 'But... but how does it work? It must be completely different from the original.'

'Not entirely. There are some changes, naturally. I've filled the case with magnetic conductors to probe for the Earth's magnetic field over a large area. That was the easy part. To create a stable time field, there has to be two forces pulling in opposite directions, suspending the traveller in time. The arch creates a strong time field and because of its size, the traveller is held in a rigid state and in close proximity to the Earth. But this clock, on the other hand, can only be used to amplify the magnetic field and pull from the Earth. That leaves me with only one option for generating the opposing pull.'

'You're going to use the moon, aren't you?' said Catherine slowly.

'Correct. That's the fundamental difference here. The moon has a dual purpose: Not only will it reflect the cosmic rays, but also it will be providing the opposing pull to generate the time field. This is not without its disadvantages and dangers, though. To guarantee success, it must be activated during a full moon... at midnight.'

'That's the time of the strongest pull.'

'Exactly! By my calculations, that pull will be powerful enough to transpose the time-traveller, hopefully travellers, through time. I finished it two weeks ago, I've just been waiting for the full moon, to use it. I was going to go back in time to prevent Cornelius's fiendish plot from happening.'

'So when is the next full moon?' Catherine asked.

'Tomorrow.'

'It must be great to have your own time machine to take you to any time you want,' Jamie said. 'You could go and see the dinosaurs.'

Hector smiled. 'No, I couldn't. To go that far back in time with this device, would require the gravitational pull from a planet the size of Jupiter, at a distance of a couple of million miles away – so it's impossible. The best I can hope for with this is around 300 years.'

Catherine smiled broadly at Jamie and Todd. 'Boys – it just might be possible that you're going back to your own time, what do you think of that?'

'It's… fantastic,' said Jamie.

'Yeah, fantastic,' Todd confirmed with a grin.

Hector pulled out an iron plate from beneath the clock. He opened the door to the trunk, revealing a brass handle connected to a chain. 'The device is activated by standing on this plate and pulling down the regulator, but it will never work without this.' He drew a velvet pouch from his pocket and took out a small, cubed crystal. 'This is the crystal.' He passed it to Jamie. 'The most important component of all. It's made from a secret amalgamation of elements created by the

Xuni tribe's ancestors. The High Priest and the elders know nothing of its composition.'

'It's so heavy for such a small thing,' said Jamie, and passed it to Todd.

Todd held the inch-square crystal towards the burning wall-lamp, marvelling at the spectrum of brilliant colours. 'Amazing,' he whispered.

'It certainly is,' said Hector, taking it from him. 'Now then, I need you to tell me the exact date on which you were in the laboratory beneath the museum, I will set the device to noon of the following day, a day you haven't lived yet: you don't want to bump into yourselves, do you? That would cause a catastrophic paradox.'

Once a date had been agreed upon, Hector set the time machine. Fiddling with something behind the silver clock-face, he said, 'I'm releasing the retention valve, which means that once you've returned to your time, it will return to the fourth dimension forever, never to be seen again.'

A burst of ringing, from a bell on the wall, alerted Hector.

'Soaring eagles. That's the alarm telling me that someone's outside.' Springing into action, he rushed from the room.

They followed him to the front door. Jamie stood in the middle of the room. Only the flames in the grate moved. With sword in hand, Hector crept to the windows. Opening the curtains an inch, he whispered, 'We're in grave trouble.'

XIII

'What is it, Hector?' whispered Catherine.

'Cornelius is here. And there are at least three carriages outside.' He spun round, pointing the sword at Jamie and Todd. 'You've brought them to me, haven't you?'

Todd's tongue flicked his chipped tooth. 'No we haven't, honest.'

'Of course they haven't,' Catherine scolded.

A sudden burst of knocking on the door made Jamie jump. Hector remained still, evidently thinking out his next move, but at the sound of a heavy thud against the door, he moved quickly, running to the windows and pulling down on a wooden lever - only to have it snap in his hands. 'Blast!' he cried, 'the rigging hasn't discharged.'

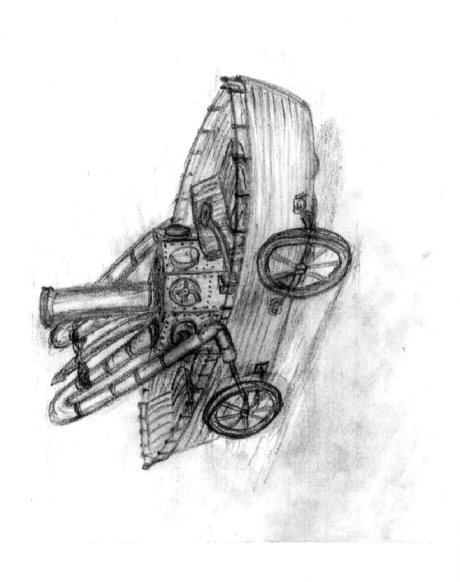

'Oh, Hector,' Catherine wailed, 'please don't tell me this is another of your mad schemes that hasn't worked!'

Another crashing blow hit the door, prompting Hector to grab the rubber tubing Todd had sat on earlier, and rush to the water main. As he fixed the metal connector to the protruding main, the battering ram crashed into the door yet again, peppering the floor with splinters of wood.

'Catherine, take over here.' Desperately, Hector explained the dial which regulated the water. The door took another heavy blow, which almost split it in two. 'Turn the dial, now!' Hector cried, standing close to her.

Catherine released a powerful jet of water just as the door came crashing from its hinges, revealing a group of dark figures in the doorway. She pointed the nozzle at them with devastating effect. The water shot out in torrents, repelling the intruders.

'That's it, Catherine, just keep them back.'

Suddenly, everyone froze at the sound of breaking glass. A heavy object had been thrown at the windows, but iron bars fitted in front of the curtains stopped it entering the room. 'Keep them at bay, Catherine, just for a couple of minutes!' Hector urged, before ordering Jamie and Todd, 'Follow me!'

Hector was first to reach the lab. He snatched the blanket from the grandfather clock and spread it on the floor, then struggled to lay the heavy clock down on the blanket. 'This is too heavy for you to carry because of the magnets, so drag it out to the back yard on this. I'll meet you there.'

He vanished, leaving Jamie to take one corner of the blanket and Todd the other.

'It weighs a ton,' groaned Todd, slipping on the carpet.

'We *must* get this to the back yard,' said Jamie, as he heaved on his corner. 'It's our ticket home.'

With their next effort, they got the clock moving across the room. Success spurred them on and they reached the doorway, but then had difficulty negotiating the turn.

'Get behind it, Todd, and push,' said Jamie.

With Todd pushing the clock and Jamie tugging at the blanket, the large timepiece was soon on the move again. They slid it down the passageway on the polished floorboards, towards a door which opened onto the yard. In the doorway, Todd paused to stand upright and groaned. 'I've got mental cramp in my legs and back!'

A loud explosion in a large shed nearby made them both jump. It was quickly followed by another explosion, then another.

'You all right, Todd?' asked Jamie, with a worried glance.

Todd rubbed his back. 'Yeah, but what the hell d'you think that was?'

Before Jamie could reply, a loud hissing, followed by slow beats, gaining momentum, came from the shed. 'I don't know what *they* were, but *that* must be Hector's steam thing,' he said. 'Come on, let's get this into the yard. Are you OK to carry on?'

Todd nodded. Renewing their efforts, they dragged the time machine out of the house and onto stone paving slabs. The sound of a steam engine, now in full flow, made them pull harder. As they reached the shed, they saw a strange contraption slowly emerging. Although it was dark, Jamie could make out the outline of a rowing boat fixed to big iron wheels. An engine block with a tall funnel completed the peculiar sight. Hector jumped off and hurried over to them. Jamie sighed with relief at the sight of him.

'Come on, boys!' Hector shouted, grabbing two corners of the blanket. 'I don't think Catherine can hold them for much longer. We must get away from here, and quickly.'

His desperate words urged Jamie and Todd on. Twisting the corners of the blanket tightly, they hauled the clock onto the vehicle.

'Well done. Now get on board,' urged Hector. 'My case! I've left it in the shed.' He then ran off.

A sudden scream came from inside the house.

'It's Catherine!' cried Jamie. 'Quick, give me the catapult.'

Todd tossed him the weapon. Catching it deftly, Jamie dashed into the house, and raced along the passageway. Catherine was cowering against the wall, still holding the hose. 'The water's stopped! They'll be in here any second!' she gasped.

Jamie already had the catapult loaded with one of the stones from his stash. As a dark figure appeared in the doorway, he let fly, aiming the missile at the intruder's chest. He quickly reloaded and picked off another invader, before turning sharply and running from the house with Catherine. Hector met them outside.

'We have to go, Hector!' Jamie cried, as he and Catherine clambered aboard. 'They're coming!'

Footsteps echoed along the floorboards in the passageway. Hector reached into the case by his side, took out a couple of bottles and handed them to Jamie and Todd. 'Here, throw these at them, they will only stun.'

Jamie and Todd hurled the glass missiles in the direction of the back door. A moment later they heard glass breaking, but no explosion. 'They didn't go off!' Jamie howled, exchanging a worried look with Todd.

Hector snapped into action as the stampede left the house. 'Brace yourselves; we're going to smash through the gates.'

Fearing for his safety, Jamie crouched in his seat. Hector turned a gauge, which let out a loud hissing, and picked up some reins. He then released a lever and the steam vehicle shuddered into motion, accelerating towards the wooden gates. Jamie held on grimly. The impact was fierce and sent the two gates flying, and bolts and splinters of wood spraying through the air. Hector struggled with the reins.

Dark figures were scattered outside the house and when someone shouted, announcing that it was Hector, more emerged from the fog. Jamie noticed three parked carriages partially hidden in the fog. Suddenly, a man drew close,. Catherine let out a scream. Jamie fired a stone at close range; the man groaned and staggered back.

'We're going to crash into the houses opposite!' Catherine cried.

Hector stood up and had to use all his might pulling on the reins, manoeuvring the contraption. Negotiating the turn, he twisted the gauge for more pressure, accelerating on the uneven road.

Jamie gasped as the three carriages, each pulled by four horses, set off in pursuit. 'They're after us,' he shouted.

'Throw the stun bombs at them!' Hector ordered, his hair flapping in the wind whilst he gripped the controls.

'But they don't work.'

'Just try the others!'

Jamie jabbed his finger at his temple, indicating Hector's insanity, then he and Todd rummaged through the case, as the contraption rocked from side to side. They extracted small bottles full of liquid, but all were launched to the same negative effect.

Catherine screamed for Hector to do something.

Moments later, a voice from one of the carriages threatened, 'Stop, or we'll shoot!'

Catherine's face was a mask of horror. 'Stop, Hector, they're going to open fire.'

'Never!' Hector turned the gauge, creating more speed and more smoke from the tall funnel.

A shot rang out.

Hector ordered Todd to take the reins.

'Me?' Todd replied, edging back.

'For heaven's sake, boy, do as he says!' Catherine shouted.

Reluctantly, Todd took control whilst Hector rifled through the case and retrieved a foot-long tube, with a short fuse at one end. He struck a match and lit the fuse as another shot whizzed past his ear. He ducked as the fuse sparked into life. Thick black smoke poured from the tube as Hector waved it to and fro; in a matter of seconds, their pursuers disappeared behind a cloud of acrid, black smoke.

'Well done, Hector,' said Catherine.

'How do I slow this thing down?' Todd shouted. 'Quick! Tell me what to do!'

They were nearing a T-junction, where a brick wall rose in front of them. Hector dropped the spent tube overboard and took the reins from Todd, but didn't have time to reduce speed. He pulled hard, and the vehicle flipped up on two wheels. Jamie was horrified to see the cobbled stones so close. Hector roared at everyone to lean to one side, and they crashed back down onto all four wheels.

Jamie knew how close they had come to rolling over, though Hector didn't seem fazed. 'Why didn't you use a steering wheel?' Jamie asked.

'A what?'

'A steering wheel, it would give you much more control.'

Hector spoke over his shoulder. 'Sounds good, but I think this is not the time to change the steering mechanism. Now we have the problem of where we're going to keep the time machine until tomorrow night.'

'What about your house in Bedford Square?' Todd suggested.

'You know, that's not such a bad idea. Cornelius doesn't know I've made a time machine. If we make it to Bedford Square, we could unload it and hide it somewhere.' He turned the gauge, further increasing the speed. 'There's not a moment to lose; it's only a matter of time before Cornelius comes to the house.'

The iron wheels screeched and clanked over the cobbles on the road leading to London Bridge. As they crossed the Thames, the engine began to labour, making strange stuttering noises, which grew steadily louder. The intense heat coming from the engine-block alarmed Jamie, and the severe vibrations, which shook his very bones, added to his worries.

By the time they entered The Strand, there was clearly a problem with the contraption. It shook violently, and the smoke pouring from the funnel was black and thick. Hector dismissed Catherine's advice to slow down. He told her Cornelius was probably racing to the house at that very moment, then applied more pressure to the over-worked engine. Jamie kept a worried eye on the billowing smoke.

As they roared into Bedford Square, their vehicle was shuddering out of control. When they pulled up outside the house, Hector was unable to cut off the engine.

He grabbed his case and jumped from the vehicle. 'We must get the time machine inside before this thing blows!' he shouted. He handed Catherine the case and a key. 'Open the door, quickly,' he told her.

By now, the engine-block was shaking furiously. Jamie feared an explosion at any moment. He, Hector and Todd put all their might into lifting the clock-case. They dragged it towards the house only moments before the engine finally exploded, sending the funnel high into the air and the wheels flying off in all directions.

'Get inside!' Hector shouted, as pieces of iron rained down onto the road.

They hauled the cumbersome time machine down the hall and into the back room, then together they heaved it upright into a corner.

'This will have to do, here,' said Hector, 'we must leave immediately.'

'Where are we going?' Catherine asked, as they ran from the house, avoiding scattered debris from the steam contraption. 'It's the middle of the night.'

About to reply, Hector stopped, and cocked his head to listen.

'What is it?' Catherine whispered.

He turned his head and met her eyes. 'Horses,' he said, frowning. Moments later, the air rang with the sound of horses' hooves, charging towards them from beyond the fog. 'We must go!' he cried. 'When they discover the house is empty, they'll search the whole area. Later, we must go back to make sure the time machine is safe. But that will have to wait; in the meantime we must seek refuge.'

They soon came to a wide street. 'This is New Oxford Street, isn't it?' said Todd. 'Why don't we go to the hideout?'

Jamie nodded and spoke to Hector. 'We know where we can hide for the night, but I think we'll have to make up a story to get in.'

'Then lead the way, dear boy.'

***

Hector and Catherine both looked decidedly over-dressed in the room where Henry Holton held court.

Billy emerged from the shadows and gasped with surprise. 'Todd? Jamie? 'enry, it's Todd and Jamie.'

Henry glimpsed them, half-hidden in the darkness, and glared. 'What is goin' on 'ere?' The gang-leader spat on the floor. 'I fawt you two got arrested.'

'How did *you* get away from the Peelers?' Swiper asked.

Todd described how they had both escaped and made it to the church.

'How did you get away, Swiper?' Jamie wanted to know.

'I climbed out of a back window and shimmied down the drainpipe.' He shook his head. 'I can't believe the way you acted when the Peelers turned up.'

'What about Patch - did he get away?' Jamie asked.

Swiper sucked on his long stemmed pipe. 'Yeah, 'e got away. 'e's out on a job.'

Henry's hard features gave way to a grin. 'Let that be a lesson, Todd.' He turned to Hector with narrowed eyes, and asked, 'So who are you?'

'I'm Jamie's uncle.' Hector replied, sticking to their story.

Henry's stare fell on Catherine. 'I'm the maid of the house,' she explained.

Jamie stepped forward. 'Henry, this is my Uncle Hector that I told you about; you know, we lost him the other day.' Henry nodded slightly. 'We were reunited earlier today and tonight we went out for a meal. After we left the restaurant, a gang tried to rob us. They chased us and, as we were so close, I thought it was a good idea to come here.'

Henry got to his feet. 'We'll get 'em for ya.'

Jamie couldn't believe that Henry was prepared to go to such lengths. He finally realised that Henry had embraced him and Todd. He shook his head. 'No, no need, but could we stay here for the night?'

'Of course you can stay, you're all welcome. Make yourselves at 'ome.'

Hector reached for his pocket watch. 'All right, which thief has my watch?' His angry question went unanswered. 'I want my watch returned at once, or else.'

Henry rose from his seat again, sneering. 'Or else you'll do what?'

'I'll destroy this rat-infested pit.'

'Please, Henry,' said Jamie, nearing the desk, 'No trouble, please.'

The gang-leader waved Jamie away. 'Grab 'im,' he commanded, jerking his chin at Hector.

Gang members moved swiftly, but Hector quickly put his case down, sprung it open and brought out a miniature pair of bellows. Almost instantly, he filled the immediate area with fine dust, disabling the young men who were reduced to coughs and splutters. This gave him time to draw out a steel rod, which opened telescopically into a sword with a hand guard. Hector lunged towards Henry, resting the makeshift weapon's sharp end on the gang-leader's chest. 'If anyone moves, I swear, I'll run him through,' Hector threatened, with eyes blazing.

The whole room froze. Henry's expression was hard; his eyes flicked down briefly at the steel that flashed under the oil lamps, then back to Hector. 'Right, who's got 'is watch?' said Henry in a measured voice.

Several tense moments passed, until Hawk owned up to taking it.

'Well then 'and it back to 'im, will ya?' Henry ordered, his voice rising.

His timepiece restored, Hector removed the sword from Henry's chest. 'It has sentimental value, you see. Now then, I will pay you for letting us stay the night.'

Henry couldn't hide his surprise at the large, white £5 note in Hector's hand, but was quick to take the money.

'What is it you do, 'ector?' he asked.

'I... work for the Government, but it's all very confidential.' Hector swigged from a bottle he'd been offered.

Jamie sighed heavily and whispered to Todd, 'For a minute back then I thought it was going to get really bad.'

Todd nodded. 'Hmm, me too, but you've got to hand it to Hector. He's pretty cool. He's not afraid of anyone.'

Catherine moved close to Jamie. 'I haven't yet thanked you for saving me earlier, it was incredibly courageous.' And then, she planted a kiss on his cheek. Her lips were the softest thing Jamie had ever experienced. He felt himself blush.

'You're a right little hero, aren't you, Jamie?' said Todd scornfully, as the two of them moved to a darkened part of the room.

Jamie couldn't conceal a smile. 'What's wrong? Jealous?'

'I've just had a thought about Hector,' Todd continued, ignoring Jamie's remark.

'And?'

Todd hesitated. 'I know he's a cool guy and everything, but haven't you noticed: almost everything he's made is rubbish?'

'Like what? The smoke-screen worked.'

'Yeah, and that's about the only thing. When we was at the house there was that lever that snapped when he tried to launch the rigging. Then there was the high-pressure water hose that broke down, and his magnesium lantern didn't last. The stun bombs didn't work and what about his... what d'ya call it? Steam carriage express. It blew to smithereens.'

Jamie laughed. 'That was an amazing thing, wasn't it?'

Todd's stare was intense. 'But don't you see? That time machine he's made, how do we know it's going to work? We could disappear into thin air.'

He was right! Jamie's happy mood vanished along with the memory of Catherine's kiss. He looked over to where Hector sat, and bit his lip. 'Oh my God, you're right. What are we going to do?'

Todd shrugged. 'What can we do? If we want to live in *our* time again, what choice do we have?'

***

Jamie stirred from a deep sleep; someone was nudging him gently. His eyes opened to almost total darkness; the oil lamps were turned down low.

He recognised Hector's voice. 'Jamie, I have to talk with you.'

He shifted onto his elbows, unable to see Hector's face. The room was quiet but for some snoring some way off. 'What is it?' he asked, rubbing his eyes.

'Jamie, in your time, are you familiar with... cholera?'

'Cholera? No.'

'That's good; that means it's been eradicated. Listen carefully, I have some very bad news. Todd has cholera.'

'What?' Jamie asked, not knowing what cholera was exactly, but aware that it was something serious.

'He has all the symptoms, I'm afraid; sickness and diarrhoea, cramp and a huge thirst. It can be contracted within 24 to 48 hours, from contaminated food and water. Todd must get back to your time where he can be properly treated. Cholera is a grave illness, Jamie.'

Jamie gasped, unable to believe what he was hearing. Was this a bad dream? His eyes had adjusted to the darkness, and he could just make out Hector's silhouette. 'What's going to happen to him?'

'It's not possible to take him to a doctor here, what with the situation we're in, but if he gets back to your time he will be fine, I'm sure. But the longer it goes untreated the greater the danger he might die.'

'Oh, no,' Jamie whispered.

'When we go back to the house in the morning, I'll give Todd something to stop the sickness and diarrhoea, and he needs to drink plenty of water. But over the next 12 hours he could deteriorate. His cramp will probably worsen.

'We must not let on to him about this. Lord knows how he would react to such news. Catherine is also aware. I'm sorry to burden you with this, but now it's become a matter of life and death that you return to your time.' Hector patted Jamie's arm and melted into the darkness.

XIV

The following morning, as Jamie stood in the hideout, his eyes were heavy and his head was pounding; he had hardly slept after Hector's dreadful revelation. How was he ever going to keep such appalling news to himself? Now they *had* to get back; Todd's life depended on it.

Most of the gang members were gathered around.

Henry smiled and shook Hector's hand, 'So long, old man. Loved the story when you 'ad to dress as Burmese soldiers to escape a massacre, only to bump into the British Army.' There were rumbles of laughter. 'You're a courageous man, Hector, but a little mad.'

Hector's smile was tight. 'What do you mean?'

'Who else would enter a gang's den and then threaten to kill the leader?'

'Yes, quite. Well, good-bye, Henry,' Hector said, shaking the gang leader's hand.

Jamie thought Hector's mood was rather cold, and wondered why the engineer hadn't been his buoyant self all morning. Was it because Todd was ill?

When they reached street-level, a fresh breeze greeted them.

Todd looked up at a blue sky. 'I can't believe there's no fog, *and* it's sunny.'

'It's Saturday,' Hector said. 'So the factories are less busy. This strong wind has also helped keep the fog away.' He began to walk. 'We need a cab. Come, this way.'

When Jamie saw Todd's face in daylight, he could see it had shrunk a little; some flesh seemed to have gone, making his cheekbones more prominent. The skin around his eyes was dark - and it wasn't because of the bruising.

They *had* to get back to their time.

Hector soon hailed a cab and as they approached Bedford Square, he checked the area warily. There was an air of tension in the cab. The remnants of Hector's vehicle from the night before seemed to have gone.

'45 Bedford Square,' the driver announced.

Hector told the driver to wait.

The front door to the house was damaged, and had been secured with nailed planks.

'Something very heavy hit this last night, it's sheared the lock clean away,' said Hector, pulling at the planks of wood, so they could enter.

Inside the house, seeing the grandfather clock where Hector had placed it the night before, triggered Jamie's memory; the two ghosts had appeared exactly where the clock now stood.

Hector checked the mechanisms of the time machine and gave a grunt of approval.

'Hector, this will work when we use it, won't it?' Todd asked.

Hector paused. 'I hope so; otherwise you'll disappear into thin air.'

There was no concern in his words. When Catherine told him not to scare the boys, he showed no emotion. What was the matter with Hector?

'You might experience some atmospheric instability, but it should be fine,' he said.

Although Hector's mood was offish, Jamie needed to know what was in store for them. 'What's... atmospheric instability?' he asked. 'I'm not going to get another nosebleed, am I?'

'I can't guarantee that. Using the moon's gravitational pull for the opposing force makes the time field a lot weaker. As I said, the arch creates a strong and stable field, like riding on a luxury train, but this will be more like being on the roof of the train, hoping you don't come off. Nosebleeds and aching bones should be the least of your worries.' He pointed at the clock-face. 'To activate this device, the crystal, which I will give to you later, slots into this small aperture. Once the crystal is inserted you must pull out the plate and stand on it, holding hands. Do not let go. Open this door and pull down on the regulator.'

Todd hesitated. 'Hector, is this house haunted?'

'Haunted? Good heavens above, why do you ask?'

'It's just that in our own time, Jamie saw two ghosts.'

Hector frowned at Jamie. 'You saw two ghosts?'

Jamie nodded. 'In this very room, right where the clock is.'

'Well, I've never experienced any paranormal activity,' Hector said irritably. 'And I don't believe in ghosts.' He left the room for the kitchen.

'What's up with Hector?' Todd whispered.

Jamie shrugged, trying not to stare too long at Todd's sickly appearance. He cursed that he couldn't tell him about his grave illness. 'How are you feeling, now?'

'That's the third time this morning you've asked how I'm feeling. Like I said, I had the runs again last night and some bad stomach pains, but at the moment, I feel over the moon,' he told him.

Hector returned, holding a glass filled with a grey cloudy liquid, as well as what looked like an army canteen made of pewter. 'Here, drink this, Todd. It will stop the sickness and diarrhoea.'

Todd didn't hesitate; he downed the medicine in one gulp.

'Good,' Hector said, passing Todd the canteen, but for a moment, keeping a tight grip on it. 'This is very dear to me; a dying general gave it to me on the battlefield in Afghanistan. Do *not* lose it.'

Todd swallowed hard and nodded.

Jamie studied the canteen, as Hector explained to Todd that it was full of water, and he must keep himself hydrated. With its beaten appearance, the canteen certainly looked as if it *had* been in the heat of battle. Jamie guessed the slim, flat shaped vessel with its elongated screw-top could hold about a pint.

'Now then, is everyone hungry?' Hector asked. 'I think we'll have breakfast in our room at Claridge's.'

Hector waited until everyone was on the pavement before fixing the front door. 'I'm going to nail only three planks of wood to the door,' he told Jamie. 'So when you try to gain entry, it will be easy for you.'

'That seemed to go well, without any intervention by Cornelius,' said Catherine, sitting next to Hector inside the cab. 'To be honest, I was expecting him.'

The cab had joined the slow-moving traffic in New Oxford Street, and 10 minutes had passed when a sudden burst of whistles rang out.

'Whatever is all the fuss?' said Hector, peering from the window.

Jamie spotted a policeman halting the on-coming traffic. More police appeared.

'What's happening?' Catherine asked.

'Don't know,' Hector replied thoughtfully.

A loud voice gave an order to halt. The carriage stopped abruptly. 'We have reason to believe this vehicle has been used in a crime.'

'What you talking about?' growled the driver. 'There must be some mistake.'

'No sir, your licence number matches a number reported to a crime. Will you step down, please, sir?'

Just then the door beside Hector's seat opened to reveal two policemen. 'Could you step outside, please, sir?'

'What on earth do you want with me?' Hector asked with a disbelieving frown. 'I have done nothing wrong; I'm just a passenger.'

'We have to check the occupants as well.' The policemen spoke to Catherine. 'Could you accompany us, please, ma'am?'

Hector and Catherine stepped into the street.

'They're leading them away,' said Todd, at the window. 'I wonder what's going on.'

The door on the boys' side of the carriage opened, startling them. A man with a familiar, smiling face took a seat opposite them. Jamie recognised him as Bob, the man who had rescued them the other night - *but what was he doing here*?

Todd grinned. 'I recognise you from the other night. You're Bob, aren't you?'

The man crossed his legs, removed his bowler hat and ran his fingers through his short, wavy hair. 'No, I'm not... my name is Cornelius.'

Jamie and Todd jumped up simultaneously.

'Relax,' Cornelius said, indicating that they should sit. 'We have some very important things to talk about.'

'I – I don't understand, we've heard bad things about you,' Todd said.

'I can believe that. First, let me say, I know you are from the future. Initially, we thought you were here by design, but we soon came to the conclusion that a terrible accident must have occurred to bring you here. I know what a difficult time you've had. Believe it or not, a massive operation to find you has been in place since you ran away from the museum. You've been followed ever since, with much diligence.'

Jamie turned sharply to Todd. 'See, I told you we were being followed. And I wasn't imagining the figure in Manchester Square.'

Cornelius laughed. 'We did lose you at one point, when you went off on that omnibus. We put everyone on the streets to look for you. We found you again trying to burgle that house and were on the verge of intervening but, as you had visited Colonel Ramsbottom and Miss Wallace, I just knew you were going to lead us to Hector. We also lost you last night, but again, everyone from the organisation was on the streets.' Cornelius sat forward. 'Listen to me, boys, Hector is not what he seems. Whatever he's told you about me is lies. Hector - and possibly Catherine Wallace, too, we're not entirely sure about her - plans to travel to the future and blackmail world leaders with the threat of unleashing a deluge of diseases. He wants world domination.'

Could that be true? Jamie covered his mouth with his hand and swallowed hard. Could Hector have been lying to them all along? And Catherine, too?

'He's got that folder on diseases,' Todd said. 'You saw it, Jamie. And what about those jars and test-tubes he didn't want us near? What's in them?'

Jamie shook his head vigorously. 'No, Hector's a good man.'

'Don't be a fool, Jamie,' said Cornelius. 'I work in a big organisation in conjunction with the British and Dutch Governments. See the policemen out there? Well, they're not policemen; they are members of the organisation.' Jamie looked out. The policemen *were* real, surely. Could Cornelius be the one telling the truth? He looked back at Cornelius. *Was he* the one they should trust? Or not?

Cornelius met his eyes with a fixed stare and continued, 'Let me tell you something about Hector. When he came back from China with his wondrous discovery, I worked with him for the same cause. But all the while, he was working for his own terrible agenda. After we realised his intentions, Hector went into hiding. We left Catherine alone, but kept her under surveillance; hoping she would eventually lead us to him. We were desperate to find him, because we feared he would construct his own time-travelling device. When you met him last night, did you see him working on anything that could be a time-travelling device?'

Todd nodded.

'Wait, Todd,' said Jamie sternly. 'How do we know we can trust him?'

'You're quite right to be wary, Jamie,' Cornelius said. 'It's all right.' Turning back to Todd, he asked, 'Why did Hector go to the house at Bedford Square last night, *and* this morning?'

'Don't say anything, Todd!' Jamie snapped. They couldn't reveal everything to this man they hardly knew.

Cornelius nodded. 'Very well, I understand. Listen, I know Hector very well, so to my reckoning, he said he will let you use the device to deliver you back to your own time.' He studied their faces closely. 'Did he happen to show you a small piece of crystal, about so big? You don't have to answer that. But that piece of crystal is most vital to time-travel, and if he did say you can use the time machine, I would almost certainly say he never gave it to you.'

'You're right; he didn't give us the crystal!' Todd said.

'Shut up, Todd.'

Jamie didn't know what to believe. Could they trust Hector? Was Cornelius right? Or was he trying to trick them? His thoughts were interrupted by a uniformed agent opening the carriage door.

He shook his head at Cornelius and left.

Cornelius maintained his calm, and kept his eyes on Jamie. 'Hector doesn't have the crystal on him.' His stare unnerved Jamie. 'So now I must search you.'

'We haven't got it!,' Todd protested.

Cornelius reached across and felt around Jamie's ankles through his socks. All the while his eyes burrowed into Jamie's. Jamie kept still as his legs were searched, followed by his trouser and coat pockets.

Todd was checked in the same way. Snaking hands probed Todd's coat pockets. 'Sorry about this, but it has to be done.' Cornelius sat back in the seat. 'Hmm, what's he done with it?' he muttered. Then he noticed Hector's leather case.

He opened the case and searched it. 'I can't believe some of the things he has in here,' he grumbled. 'But I have to say, he's very inventive. It just proves how desperate he is to achieve his sinister plan.'

He put the case down and stood up. 'You two need to decide whom you are going to trust. The insane engineer whose inventions rarely function? Or a competent commander? Did you know that his CO was about to have him certified as a madman before Hector left the army? No, I didn't think so. I'd advise you to consider *very* carefully. Your lives may depend upon it.' The two boys exchanged a worried glance. 'If you want to see your families again,' Cornelius continued, 'find that crystal and give it to us. I promise I will make sure you are sent to your own time. If, or when you find the crystal, run to the side of the road and just hold it aloft. Don't worry; you will be closely followed, so someone will see you and you will be rescued. And be warned: Hector will not hesitate to inflict harm on you if his plans are threatened.'

At that, Cornelius opened the door and stepped out on to the kerb. 'I'll give you a few minutes to talk it over before I allow Hector to return. Don't worry, boys, together we'll succeed.'

When Cornelius closed the door Jamie's words clashed with Todd's. 'Let me speak!' Jamie shouted as Todd's chest heaved erratically. 'Who are we going to believe?' he continued.

Todd responded confidently. 'It's simple. Hector's some kind of mad scientist who wants to rule the world. Like Cornelius said: if Hector wants us to use the time machine, why didn't he give us the crystal? And if he hasn't got it on him, then where is it? Well, I'll tell you, he's hidden it in the house for him to collect later, so he can use the time machine instead of us.'

'No,' Jamie whispered. 'I'd never have suspected Hector of being evil, I thought he was a good person.'

'Look at the way Hector's been this morning. You know he's changed. You said that yourself. You saw that folder on diseases, and what's in them jars and test-tubes? The diseases he's going to take to the future. *Our future!*'

Jamie thought Hector's strange mood was because Todd had cholera. But he couldn't find a good reason why he would have a folder on diseases. The case against Hector was mounting. 'Let's stop and think,' he said carefully. 'We don't know what, or who, to believe now.'

Todd raised his finger and said, 'I know, if we don't find the crystal by, say, 10 o'clock tonight, we'll attract Cornelius's attention and tell him Hector has the time machine primed for midnight.'

Jamie was still unsure. 'I don't think that's a good idea.'

'I don't care what you think, I want to go home and I don't want some nutter destroying our chance.' An eager smile flashed across his face. 'I'm going to tell Cornelius about the time machine at the house right now, before Hector comes back.'

'No, Todd! We don't know if we can trust him. We need to think about this.'

'I already have,' said Todd, reaching for the door handle.

Jamie lunged at Todd, grabbing him around the neck. Now what? The boy he held in a head-lock was the same boy who had won three fights at school.

The more Todd demanded to be released, the tighter Jamie squeezed. He hoped that a bout of cramp would strike Todd but, sick or not, he thrashed and kicked his legs. Jamie couldn't hold him any longer; his grip loosened enough for Todd to bury a punch in Jamie's stomach.

Todd was free! On impulse, Jamie lashed out with a punch of his own. It connected with Todd's forehead and he fell back against the opposite seat with a shocked look. Suddenly, Todd moved towards the door, and opened it. This time, Jamie was unable to act; he stayed in the seat clutching his stomach, where he'd been punched.

The other door opened. 'Going somewhere, Todd?' Hector asked, standing on the step.

'Er... no, just trying to see where you was.'

Hector sighed. 'Catherine and I have just been accused of being involved in a robbery with the cab driver. As you can see, we are all entirely innocent. The audacity of it. As if Catherine is a wrong-doer.' Hector paused. 'That was an awfully big operation just to stop common thieves.'

'What are you implying, Hector?' asked Catherine, taking her seat at his side as the cab rocked into life.

'That entire episode could have been engineered by Cornelius,' he replied. Then, flashing a fierce glance at Jamie, he asked, 'Did anyone come into the carriage while we were away?'

Jamie shook his head, but didn't meet his eyes. Todd was frantically searching for something. Finally, he pulled the slim canteen from down between the seats where it had been stuck, and drank from it. Jamie kept his gaze on the floor, wondering if he had made a monumental mistake in stopping Todd from going to Cornelius?

***

Inside Claridge's, standing next to Hector in a queue at the reception desk, Jamie marvelled at the luxurious foyer, with its marble floor and pillars and a wealth of dark, varnished wood. A violinist played soothing music in the adjoining restaurant area.

'Is everything all right with you two?' Hector asked. 'You've both been very quiet since the police incident.'

'Can't you see they're nervous, Hector?' said Catherine. 'They must be anxious about tonight.'

'Hmm,' was all Hector said.

'Where's the crystal, Hector?' Todd asked.

'It's safe,' he replied and glanced at his watch.

Jamie viewed Hector sceptically, wondering why the scientist had asked him if cholera had been eradicated in the future. Was he really acquiring information for his dreadful plan?

'Why, if it isn't Hector Lightfoot!' The American accent made them all look round.

A tall, bearded, overweight man, in the company of two women wearing long elegant dresses and another smartly dressed man, stood before them.

Hector shuffled uncomfortably, glancing quickly around the foyer and faking a smile. 'Hello... Charles, isn't it?'

'You're damn right it is. Where have you been for the past year?' The big man shook Hector's hand and turned to his companions. 'This is Hector, the fellow I was telling you about just the other day.' Hector kissed the hands of the two women and shook the other man's hand, as Charles spoke. 'The work you achieved on the F62 Wagon Train was immense.' Hector seemed embarrassed by the admiring smiles from the two women, and clearly not happy with the unwanted attention. 'My offer still stands, you know, regarding that job in New York,' the big American continued. 'Could make you a very rich man.'

Hector smiled politely. 'Well... I'm... I'm rather comfortable right now, actually. Besides, I have commitments here. It wouldn't be possible now.'

'Very well, Hector, but keep it in mind. What have you been doing during the past 12 months?'

Todd took the canteen from his coat. It slipped from his fingers and dropped to the floor. He retrieved it, unscrewed the top with a puzzled frown, and began exploring it. Jamie watched him, baffled. When Todd started flicking his tooth, he knew something was wrong. Then Todd grabbed his arm and pulled him to one side.

'What's wrong,' Jamie asked. Todd opened his palm, revealing the crystal. Jamie gasped. 'What... what are *you* doing with it?'

'It was hidden in the lid of the water bottle, jammed behind a piece of tin. When I dropped it just then, it must have become dislodged.'

'So *what is* Hector playing at?'

'He must have known that Cornelius would make a move, and try and find this. I'm giving it to Cornelius, and you're not going to stop me.'

Jamie certainly didn't want another scrap; he knew he'd lose. And besides, Hector *wasn't* his normal self. So he agreed. 'OK, we'll walk right out, yes?' Todd nodded.

They walked briskly past Hector and Catherine. Charles and his party had left. Jamie ignored Hector's frown, and hurried towards the exit. Once on the pavement, Todd raised his hand in the air, revealing the crystal.

'Hector's coming!' Jamie shouted, glimpsing him at the hotel doors.

Hector came out of the hotel with Catherine. 'What *are* you doing, Todd?' he asked.

Todd kept his arm aloft, ignoring him.

Jamie was relieved to see Cornelius with two of his men attempting to cross the road. They waited for a gap in the traffic, then came charging over. Cornelius knocked into a man passing by and sent his top hat tumbling to the ground.

'Throw the crystal at the ground hard, Todd, so that it shatters!' Hector shouted.

Cornelius and his subordinates froze as Todd deliberated.

'If you do that, you'll never see your own time again.' Cornelius's voice was calm, but his eyes drilled into him. 'Give it to me, Todd.'

Todd stepped back. On his left, three men in greatcoats stood ready to pounce.

'What shall I do, Jamie?'

Jamie glanced at Hector and then Cornelius.

'Throw it to the ground,' Hector ordered. 'Throw it! Or we'll all be doomed.'

'Give it to me, Todd, and I promise I'll send you both back to your time and your families,' said Cornelius.

Todd gave Hector a fleeting look before holding his hand out for Cornelius to take the crystal. 'Hector hid it inside this water bottle,' he said.

Catherine gasped, as the three men grabbed Hector roughly, and pushed Jamie and Todd towards the kerb.

Cornelius smirked triumphantly at Hector, and signalled to the driver of an iron-clad carriage parked up the street.

'Get your filthy hands off me!' Catherine was struggling in the clutches of another man wearing a greatcoat. She glared at Jamie and Todd. 'You stupid boys,' she hissed.

Cornelius removed his bowler hat to scratch his head. 'Hello, Catherine, how nice to see you again.'

'You despicable man.'

Cornelius gave another smirk, evidently enjoying seeing Hector and Catherine get bundled into the secure carriage. Jamie and Todd were then shoved towards it.

'So why are we going with them?' Jamie asked, standing on the iron step. 'We helped you.'

Cornelius frowned. 'You're no use to me now.'

He then left with his men; they boarded two waiting carriages, parked by the kerb.

Todd was sent crashing onto the cold, hard seat as the iron carriage started with a jerk. Hector had covered his face with his hands, but Catherine stared coldly at them both. 'I hope you're very pleased with yourselves.'

Jamie shuffled awkwardly on the iron bench-seat. 'What's going to happen?'

Hector pulled his hands from his face. 'Woe betide mankind. Cornelius Van Huls now has the crystal.' He shook his head in defeat. 'I had it all planned: I hid the crystal in the water canteen, knowing that Cornelius would strike. We were going to stay in the hotel until tonight, when a planned diversion would have freed you to go straight to the house.'

'But you seemed different today – not like your normal self,' Jamie muttered. 'Cornelius said you, and possibly Catherine, they wasn't sure, were going to the future to threaten the world with a load of diseases.'

Hector's eyes narrowed. 'Cornelius?' He nodded ruefully. 'He spoke to you at the road-block, then.'

'But what was in those test-tubes and jars?' Todd asked.

Hector snorted. 'Diseases. I wanted to go to the future to obtain the *cures* for today's diseases, not unleash them. I told you that last night.'

Todd shook his head. 'You didn't, Hector.'

Jamie confirmed Hector's oversight.

Catherine sighed angrily, 'If we *were* going to do what Cornelius said, would I have taken you to Hector and risked everything?'

'Let's be fair to them, Catherine,' said Hector. 'Cornelius said that his people weren't sure about you. Clever, very clever.'

'But why did you act so strange today?' Todd asked. 'You gave us no choice.'

Hector conceded with a nod. 'You're right, I did act a little oddly, only because I knew we were going to fall into Cornelius's hands at Bedford Square. It's a self-defence mechanism, I suppose. I was the same when I was a soldier, before any fighting took place.'

'So what's going to happen?' Jamie asked.

Catherine glanced at Hector briefly, then said, 'The world is now doomed.'

XV

The journey through the streets of London had been uncomfortable. Not another word had been uttered inside the carriage since they left the hotel, and Hector had sat with his hands over his face the entire time.

Jamie caught a brief view of the mast and sails of a ship through a small, barred window of the carriage that let in cold air. As the convoy slowed down outside a large building, it turned right, stopping at two high, wooden gates. A man standing at the gates allowed the vehicles access to a spacious courtyard beside by the river.

Hector strained to see through the barred window, as stable-hands arrived to unhitch the horses and lead them off to the stables. 'Here comes Patterson,' he said with distaste.

'That's the man who tried to keep us at the museum,' said Jamie.

The bald, bearded man came smiling across the courtyard towards Cornelius. 'I have news of the army, Cornelius. It should be here tonight, around 10 o'clock,' he said.

Hector spun round excitedly. 'The army isn't here yet. All is not lost.'

'What army?' Todd asked.

Hector jumped up from his seat, hitting his head on the cab roof.

'Oh, Hector, are you all right?' Catherine gasped.

'Never mind that. Can't you see? All the while that army isn't here, there's still a chance.'

The iron door squeaked open. Two men stood outside holding pistols, one of them motioned to Hector to step down.

Cornelius and Patterson met Hector and the others as they crossed the yard under escort. Cornelius spoke gleefully. 'Hector, I want to show you and Catherine what your work has achieved.'

Jamie thought that the building in front, which resembled an aircraft hangar with two huge wooden doors, looked ominous. What was behind those doors?

They entered the building through a much smaller access door, and the first thing he saw was a huge iron arch at the far end. It was similar to the one beneath the British Museum, but much bigger.

Cornelius raised his arm. 'Come. Come and see.' He led the way, all the while looking admiringly at the arch. 'You had your chance to join us, Hector.'

'Yes, but I'm not insane.'

Cornelius laughed. 'What we're about to do is not mad, but a fantastic opportunity.' He turned to Patterson. 'Get the others; I'm going to communicate with Travis.'

Hector frowned. 'Travis has been sent back in time?' he asked.

'Yes, we sent him back just before you ran off with the crystal.' Cornelius shook his head with wonderment. 'Just think; Travis could be standing on this very spot in 1775.'

An elderly man was attending to the iron arch, fiddling with a control panel close to where a lever came up from the floor. Noticing Cornelius's advance, he shuffled towards him.

'Hello, Albert,' said Cornelius. 'I have the crystal at last.'

The old scientist peered through silver-rimmed glasses at the crystal in Cornelius's hand. 'Very good, sir. Everything is now primed,' he said, taking it.

Hector's tone was harsh. 'I'm appalled at you, Rothman. How can you go along with this madness?'

Patterson emerged from a room with a group of people. As they gathered before the arch, one of them - a woman wearing a fur coat whom Jamie recognised - greeted them. 'Hello, my darlings,' she smiled, then added, 'Don't look so worried.'

She explained to the other agents how she had bought Jamie and Todd coats after they were robbed of their clothes.

Cornelius spoke to a man holding large sheets of paper. 'I want you to write; *Travis, this is Cornelius, hope all is going well. The army will be dispatched shortly. Let me know the latest developments. Place your reply in the designated area.*'

As soon as the message was written, the paper was placed beneath the arch. Cornelius nodded to Albert, prompting him to place the crystal into a slot on the control panel under the agents' expectant gaze. After operating the control panel, he pulled back the lever. Instantly, the paper vanished.

Jamie's eyes widened in wonderment: this was no magic trick using mirrors or any other deception; an object had actually disappeared. Cornelius waited briefly before nodding to Albert a second time. The scientist fiddled again with the control panel and pulled back the lever; a sheet of paper materialised.

'Wow!' whispered Todd, nudging Jamie's ribs with his elbow. 'This is mental!'

Cornelius read the paper aloud, grinning. *'Everything is in place and ready for the army. Two ships have been commissioned. I await the army so we can fulfil The Grand Plan.'*

The agents clapped and cheered.

Todd tapped Hector's arm. 'What *is* The Grand Plan?'

'Let me enlighten you, Todd,' Cornelius said. 'We are sending a well-trained army, 3000 in number, through this arch, back to the year 1775. With far superior weapons, they will board two ships to America and win the war of American Independence.'

'You're mad,' Hector said.

'No, Hector - patriotic. Britain should have won that war first time round; now we have another chance with a combined British and Dutch army. Besides, New York once belonged to the Dutch. We called it New Amsterdam. You see, Todd, Jamie, when we win that war, our two countries will become very powerful.' He addressed Hector. 'With you being a military man, I'm surprised you can't see this.'

'I understand the importance of winning a war, but not going back in time to turn a defeat into a victory. It will alter all the ensuing events in history, and cause catastrophic consequences.'

Cornelius ignored Hector's words and addressed Jamie and Todd again. 'With America's gold and other rich resources, it will make Britain and the Netherlands unbeatable forever. And the civil war raging over there at the moment - that terrible, terrible war - will not take place; now that's not a bad thing, is it? The army we're sending back to 1775 will head for New York with much superior weapons. And the handguns are completely different.' He pulled out a pistol from under his coat. 'This is also American. It's a Colt Navy revolver.' He looked fondly at the ivory grips and silver barrel. 'Yes, it's a 44-calibre, firing six rounds to the American insurgents' one. Those American riflemen will be annihilated and the army will proceed to rout the rest of the colonists, going from strength to strength.'

He picked up a book at the foot of the control panel. 'This history book will describe a different outcome when the army goes back in time and wins the war. Oh, and Hector, George Washington will not be appointed Supreme Commander in 1775, because he'll be assassinated in Boston by one of my special agents. A good idea of mine, wouldn't you say?'

Hector remained stony-faced, his jaw clenched. Cornelius walked towards Albert and put his hand on his shoulder, saying, 'So the decisive battle at Yorktown which won the war for America will never happen.' Cornelius noticed Hector's gaze on the control panel. 'Don't even think about making a grab for it, Hector. You'll be killed instantly.' His voice hardened. 'Lock them up, Patterson.'

'When are you going to send me and Jamie back to our time? You promised?' asked Todd.

Cornelius frowned at him. 'If I did that, you would tell of our plans. Then, no doubt, forces would come and prevent The Grand Plan.'

'But the device under the museum doesn't work... well, not properly,' said Todd. 'So... so how will we... '

'Take them away,' ordered Cornelius, coldly.

'So the army isn't here yet?' said Hector thoughtfully, as they left the hall.

'They're on their way,' Patterson replied.

'I can see a problem with the arch,' Hector announced.

With Catherine and Todd, Jamie followed Hector towards the stone wall by the Thames, along which ran a line of gas lamps.

Hector reached the water's edge. To Patterson, he said, 'Albert Rothman is a fine scientist, but he is getting on in years. Are you sure he has the correct quantity of iron ore to accommodate an army of 3000?'

Patterson looked at him sceptically. 'What are you talking about, Lightfoot? There's nothing wrong with Albert's estimations,' he said, confidently. 'After all, they were taken from *your* calculations and multiplied accordingly.'

Hector's gaze focused on an approaching barge, carrying coal. 'Hmm, be that as it may, but has he compensated for the acceleration of gravity when dealing with such a large mass? I wouldn't want to see so many souls evaporate into the atmosphere, however wrong their intentions. I think he's going to need a magnetic counterbalance, and in my observations I didn't see one. What would you say, Catherine?'

'Come to think of it, I didn't see a magnetic counterbalance either. If such a large number were to be transported back in time, the coupling link, which deals with selecting gravity at the desired time, would overload, annihilating everyone.'

Patterson looked from one to the other. 'All right, Lightfoot, come back into the hall and tell Cornelius what you've told me.' Hector remained where he was, by the wall. 'Well, come on,' Patterson urged, angrily.

'I would love to... but I can't stay,' Hector said, as the barge passed below. To Jamie and Todd he shouted, 'Onto the barge - quickly!'

Todd climbed up at once and jumped, but Jamie remained where he was. He saw Hector's leg move as a blur, kicking the pistol from one agent's hand in martial-arts fashion, followed by a chop to the back of the man's neck. Jamie gasped at Hector's skill. He watched him spin round with another kick, aimed at the other agent's head, and send him crashing to the ground. Jamie was amazed to see the two agents fall to the ground, stunned. Although similar to when Cornelius had floored the robbers at Seven Dials, this was something else.

Hector climbed on to wall with Jamie. 'Don't worry, I'll come back for you,' he cried to Catherine.

'You're not going without me!' cried Catherine. She rushed to where Hector stood on the wall, gathered her dress and reached out for him to haul her up.

The others had already jumped, landing on the coals heaped in the barge, but Jamie hesitated. Then, fearing that Patterson would urge the fallen agents to get up and grab him, he launched himself.

He landed, rolling down the heap of coal and out of sight of Patterson and the two agents, and found himself staring up at blue sky. The steam engine chuffed at the rear of the vessel, and they were soon some way down the river.

'Where did you learn to fight like that, Hector?' Jamie asked. 'That was awesome!'

Hector patted coal dust from his sleeves. 'I learnt many things during my stay with the Xuni Tribe, and unarmed combat was one of them.'

Todd looked down at his own hands and clothes which were also covered in coal dust. 'We've escaped Cornelius, but how are we going to escape from this?'

'We haven't escaped Cornelius,' Hector replied. 'By my reckoning, he's setting out to apprehend us right now.'

'So why did we jump into this barge?'

'Because there's always the chance that we *might* get away.'

'So an army with better weapons is going back to win the American War of Independence?' said Jamie, scratching his head. 'It's unbelievable.'

'Hmm,' confirmed Hector. 'The Brown Bess Flintlock muskets the colonists use will be no match for the seven-shot Spencer rifles the army will use. It's a far superior weapon to the musket's single shot.'

Just then, the engine slowed.

'I do believe this barge is docking in,' said Hector.

Three faces ingrained with coal dust peered over the top of the container at that moment.

'Hello,' said Hector, brightly. 'We thought we would drop in.'

The three bargemen exchanged baffled looks, then looked back at the stowaways.

Hector got unsteadily to his feet and told the others, 'We must get away from this area at once.'

***

They clambered onto a wooden jetty protruding from a wharf, while the high tide sloshed around the beams supporting it.

Hector was first ashore. He weaved his way through a small crowd of confused dockers and porters waiting to unload the barge, and was still in front, hurrying along at street level, as they left the busy docks. They were proceeding down a quiet cobbled street flanked by alleyways when, without warning, Hector came to a juddering halt, clutching his back.

'What is it, Hector?' Catherine asked, staring. 'What's wrong?'

Hector straightened slowly. 'An old war wound. I must have aggravated it. I'll be all right in a moment or two.'

A carriage pulled up on the main thoroughfare ahead of them. Jamie watched as two men in greatcoats, holding rifles, climbed out. He grabbed Hector's arm in alarm. 'Look.'

'They were quicker than I expected,' said Hector, closing his eyes and sighing heavily.

Todd looked frantically back over his shoulder. 'Can't we make a run for it? We could get on another boat, couldn't we?'

'Not this time, boy,' said Hector, shaking his head slowly.

They heard the sound of charging hooves coming from the top of the street. Moments later, a single horse and rider appeared and raced past the parked carriage.

It was Cornelius. His horse slid to a halt and Cornelius dismounted, showman-like, in one leap. The two armed agents advanced to flank him.

Cornelius shook his head with displeasure. 'Hector, Hector, what am I to do with you? Your outrageous actions put me in a difficult position. I cannot have you on the loose when The Grand Plan is imminent. It worries me.'

Catherine stepped forward, and demanded angrily, 'Why don't you leave us alone? You have the crystal.'

Cornelius faked a smile. 'Whilst Hector is alive, I won't be able to rest.'

He produced a pistol from inside his coat.

'No!' Catherine gasped.

Cornelius did not hesitate. Aiming at Hector's chest, he fired a shot.

Hector jolted backwards with a startled look. Another shot rang out; it, too, hit him in the chest. When Cornelius fired a third, Hector twisted then fell face down on the ground. As he did so, Catherine gave a high-pitched scream.

XVI

Cornelius calmly put the pistol away, as Catherine fell to her knees and sobbed over the fallen engineer. 'It had to be done, he was too dangerous,' he told her. He swung onto his horse. 'You are all free to go, but let me give this warning: if any of you attempt to impede The Grand Plan, I will not hesitate to use my gun again.' He yanked the reins and galloped away.

The two agents followed in the carriage.

Jamie stood dazed, listening to Catherine's wailing. She was kissing the back of Hector's head as Todd whispered in Jamie's ear. 'That's us done for.'

'Don't be so selfish,' Jamie snapped. 'He was a great man, I really liked him.'

Todd turned away and drank the last of the water from the canteen.

Catherine now had her arms around Hector's body. 'Oh Hector, I did love you, I did,' she wept.

Jamie stepped away, closing his eyes. Listening to Catherine tell Hector she would have married him was too much to bear. He couldn't believe that this brave man, who had fought for Queen and country in the heat of battle in foreign lands, had been killed here in London by a psychopath with mad intentions.

But Todd was right, they *were* done for. What would become of them? And what was going to happen to the world, now that Cornelius had the crystal - and The Grand Plan ready to roll? One thing was certain; they weren't going home.

'I've just thought,' Todd said. 'What's going to happen to the world now?'

'I don't know.' Not only were they stranded in a strange existence, but the consequences of what was about to happen could not be foretold. 'We'll just have to wait – ' What was going to happen to *Todd?* That was a more immediate worry. Jamie knew he would have to tell him now, so that they could get to a doctor - but could Victorian medicine save him, after so much time had elapsed? Perhaps Catherine would help.

Jamie stared down at the cobbles, wondering how he was going to break the news to Todd, but a familiar, upbeat voice made him look up. 'Yes, I promise; don't worry.'

Not another ghost! How could it be? Jamie looked up, then grinned broadly at the sight of Hector standing next to Catherine, and holding her hand.

'I've been wearing a bullet-protection garment under my clothes ever since I went into hiding,' he explained. 'It's just something I put together, from leather, chain mail, and some other materials. It's rather, er, *cool,* wouldn't you say, boys?'

'Definitely,' Todd replied, his gaunt, darkened face beaming.

Catherine feigned anger. 'I can't believe he let me think he was dead.'

Hector winked at Jamie and Todd. 'I was enjoying the cuddles and the kisses too much to let on that I wasn't! And by the way, I have an announcement to make: Catherine and I are to be married.'

'Nice one,' said Todd.

'Though we must retrieve the crystal first, or there won't be a wedding,' Hector added. 'If Cornelius has his way, the world will end in disaster.'

'What was the promise you just made, Hector?' Jamie asked.

'Oh, that. Catherine will only marry me on one condition; that I abandon my delusions of time-travel. Right now, though, we must thwart The Grand Plan!'

'Why don't we go to the police?' Todd suggested.

Hector shook his head. 'We have only hours to save this world, the police would just complicate matters. Cornelius has an army, but where's mine?' Then, a wry smile appeared. 'Actually, I do know of an army I can use.'

'Who?' Todd asked.

'You'll see.' Hector hurried towards the high road, stating, 'I have one big advantage: Cornelius thinks I'm dead. All I need now is a plan.'

***

His water bottle now empty, Todd's stomach pains returned. He was dehydrating rapidly and in desperate need of replenishment.

Swiper, the expert housebreaker, led Hector and the others through the familiar underground passageways to Henry's criminal chamber. As they arrived, the gang leader left his desk and strode towards them, glaring. He met Hector in the middle of the room. 'What the 'ell you doing, turning up at this time of day? Anyone could 'ave seen ya.' He turned to the boys and Jamie wilted under his glare. 'You two know not to come 'ere in daylight. And there's not even any fog!'

'We made sure no one saw us, don't worry. We are here for a very important reason,' said Hector calmly.

'What is it?' Henry snapped. 'Tell me!'

'Firstly, Todd needs water. Have you got any?'

'Why, what's wrong wiv 'im?' asked Henry.

'He's dehydrating. Have you got any?'

Henry called across the room. 'Mar, get Todd some water.'

As Henry's mother led Todd away, Hector asked, 'Is there somewhere that we can talk - privately?'

Henry picked up an oil lamp and headed for an adjoining storage room. Catherine followed, so Jamie tagged along, too. Surrounded by darkness, they were cocooned in the glow from the lamp, which Henry set on a battered old table.

Hector stared directly at the gang leader. 'How would you like to have enough money to leave here, and never again have to worry about this hideout being discovered? Enough money to end your criminal activities forever?'

Henry held out his hand. 'Yes, please.'

Hector ignored the hand. 'Now, you know an opportunity like that only comes at a price.'

Henry's eye's narrowed. 'Go on.'

'I need your help on a mission fraught with danger. It's possible that you, and some of your gang, might not survive. I'm offering £100.'

Henry licked his lips and swallowed. 'That's a lot of money. What do we 'ave to do, steal the Crown Jewels?'

'Remember I told you I worked for the Government?' Hector replied. 'Well, there's a renegade Government agent who has something of mine. It's located in Lower Thames Street, guarded by armed men. It must be recovered tonight.'

'I'll do it,' said Henry. 'Where's the money?'

Hector pulled out his wallet. 'I like your eagerness, but I must stress the dangers involved.' He counted out the notes under his nose. 'As I've said, they have guns – '

Henry took the bundle of notes and picked up the lamp. 'For £100 I *would* consider stealing the Crown Jewels. Let's tell the uvvers.'

The gang-leader left the room with a bounce in his step and called for the gang's attention. ''ector 'ere, wants our 'elp and 'e's paying us good money.'

Swiper removed the pipe from his mouth. 'What do we 'ave to do, 'enry?'

Henry spread the large white £5 bank notes and fanned his face to gasps and mutterings. ''ector needs our 'elp getting back somefing that belongs to 'im.'

Swiper blew out smoke through his nose. 'It must be some task 'e's asking. You've got a fortune there.'

'Sounds too good to be true,' said Zad, frowning.

Hector stepped in. 'I'm not going to lie to you. I've already told Henry, what I ask of you, *is* a dangerous task.'

'What is it den?' Zad demanded.

Hector pulled open his coat to reveal the three gunshot holes. 'My bullet-protection garment saved me earlier, when I crossed swords with them.' He then went on to tell them about the task.

The bearded J.T. leaned against one of the building's support columns, arms folded, and growled, 'So the people in this government building 'ave guns?'

'Yes, they do.'

'Then it ain't worff it, it's way too risky. If some of us get caught, or even killed, it would be the end of us 'ere.'

Henry strolled over to him, holding out a £5 note. 'Take it. You're a good man for a job like this, I want you wiv us tonight.'

The big man's eyes blazed with anger, but he wanted the money too much to refuse. He pocketed the note hastily before growling at Hector, 'So are you going to give us *all* bullet-protection garments?'

'There's not enough time. Besides, I can't get the special material needed. Just wear thick clothing and heavy coats.'

Henry pointed at Jamie. 'Did you know young Jamie's an expert wiv the sling-shot? He could be some help.'

Jamie gulped. What if he lost his nerve? Would he even be able to shoot the catapult?

'Oh, yes,' said Hector. 'Catherine mentioned his talent. Hmm, I think he could fit into my plans.' He looked at Jamie questioningly. 'Would you be prepared to be involved tonight?'

Jamie replied in a dry whisper. 'I think so.'

'Splendid.'

'I wanna be involved, an' all,' said a young voice. It was Billy.

Henry shook his head. 'No, Bill. You're doing that job with Patch in 'olborn tonight.'

The youngster stomped away, cursing.

'Do you 'ave transport?' Henry asked Hector.

'Yes, I have a hackney carriage stabled at Neal's Yard.'

Henry smiled. 'Sounds good.'

Hector had bought the carriage from the driver shortly after his 'resurrection'. He had paid handsomely for the vehicle - at which the driver had been so happy that he'd done a little jig.

Hector stroked his chin. 'Which reminds me, I need a Trojan horse.'

Henry frowned. 'What's that, a new breed?'

A smile grew on Hector's lips. 'The Greeks were at war with the Trojans, who had to use cunning to breach their barricades. They built a giant wooden horse that could hold an army. So when the curious Trojans brought it inside their fort, they were done for. Also, I must visit a pharmacist, as I plan to go with a bang.'

XVII

Lower Thames Street was cold and quiet under a bright, full moon against an inky sky. Visibility was good. The moon had arrived on cue; all would go according to plan as long as Hector could retrieve the crystal, and deliver the boys to the house before the stroke of midnight.

At nine o'clock, the clip-clopping of horses' hooves approached from an easterly direction. This clear and fogless night revealed two vehicles; a carriage and a cart. The cart was pulled by a large shire horse that lumbered slowly, casting its shadow on the cobbled road. Opposite the Tower of London, it parted company with the carriage. Catherine, who had been driving the carriage, parked it and waited, hunched in the driver's seat, wearing a heavy coat and scarf. The cart continued, with the Holton gang crowded onto it and Hector at the reins. He wore scruffy clothes, a floppy hat and a false ginger beard which sprouted out wildly.

Hector manoeuvred the one-horse cart towards the gates of the government building and stopped when a man emerged from the gatehouse. As he approached the cart, he appeared to be reading the legend *Murphy's Gas Maintenance* which was painted in white on its wooden side panels. 'What do you want?' he demanded.

Hector stood up and spoke in a loud Irish accent. 'Good evening, sir.' Sniggers from the gang were drowned out by his loud voice. 'Der appears to be a problem wit' your gas mains. Der's no gas getting troo to the premises next door.'

'Can't you come back tomorrow?'

'No sir. If we don't see to it tonight, you'll be without gas very soon. It's an emergency. Oi have papers to deal with it immediately.'

The man sighed. 'Wait there.'

Once the gateman had gone inside, Hector glared over his shoulder. 'What are you doing, laughing? At this rate, we'll be discovered before we can even get into the place.'

Henry struggled to keep a straight face and said, 'Seeing you like this and wiv that voice, it's... 'ilarious.' More sniggers and titters followed.

'Does your friend at the featre 'ave many more disguises?' Swiper inquired.

'Why do you ask?' Hector said, repositioning the bushy beard.

''cause when we next go out on a job, the disguises will come in 'andy.'

'Have you forgotten already? That after tonight, you won't have to go burgling again.'

Swiper laughed. 'Yeah, I did. Old 'abits die 'ard.'

Zad leaned forward and said, 'So what are we going to do wid de money?'

'I 'aven't fawt about it yet,' Henry replied. 'We could start a business.'

'I worked for a blacksmith's once,' Philip said, 'I know how to shoe horses.'

'Sounds like too much 'ard work, if you ask me,' J.T. grumbled. 'All that 'eat and iron.'

'I've always wanted to run a brewery,' said Swiper.

J.T. grunted his approval. 'Now that's a good idea.'

Hector sighed and spoke irritably. 'Could you lads lay off planning your futures? You're supposed to be helping me. Now is everyone sure about what they have to do?' There were nods all round. Suddenly, Hector raised his hand. 'Shhh.'

'What's this about a problem with our gas main?' asked Cornelius stepping close to the cart.

'Er, dat's right, sir,' Hector replied.

'But we have gas. Our lights are working perfectly.'

'Dat can happen, sir, but der is a loss of pressure wit' your mains going into next door and beyond.'

Cornelius sighed. 'Can't you come back in the morning? I have some important business to attend to tonight.'

'Dat's not a good idea, sir. If it's a bad leak, a build-up of gas could prove disastrous.'

'Well, I haven't smelt gas.'

'Ah, but de gas is probably trapped underground you see, sir, and one spark could blow dis place to Kingdom Come.'

Cornelius shook his head. 'No, I'm sorry, I can't allow you in. I'll take my chances. Come back tomorrow.' He walked back to the gate.

'Dat's not a good idea, sir. I have de power to summon de constabulary and der could be police swarming everywhere in t'irty minutes. You could be forced to shut down.'

'All right,' Cornelius told the gateman with an exasperated sigh, 'let them in.'

Hector drove through the entrance. Scanning the yard, he spotted Patterson joining Cornelius. They watched him halt, 50 yards from the huge doors to the hall.

Hector jumped off the cart. 'Right lads, let's get dis sorted out.' He unrolled a sheet of paper and said, 'De main line runs approximately here.'

Swiper grabbed a pickaxe, as did Philip and Henry. Zad and J.T. lit oil lamps and placed them on the ground where Hector stood.

'Dat's grand,' said Hector, eying Cornelius conversing with Patterson. When they finally walked off, Hector sided up to Hawk and spoke in a low voice. 'Right, go and do what you're good at.'

The pickpocket nodded and walked towards the gatehouse.

***

Once the Holton gang were busy pulling up the cobbles, Hector opened a leather case and brought out a handful of test-tubes sealed with corks. He lifted a large blanket coated with coal dust, to reveal Jamie lying next to Todd, rigid with apprehension. 'How's my mood?' Hector asked. 'Not so tense this time, eh?' He didn't get a reply. Hector handed Todd the test-tubes. 'Take these. If or when they're needed, feed them to

Jamie. Jamie, as I said before, fire them using your catapult, they will explode, but only stun.'

'You said that last time, but nothing happened,' Jamie said.

Hector smiled ruefully. 'I've rectified the problem. Believe me, these will work, and I've made them louder for maximum effect. Stay calm; everything should work out fine.'

'What if I break one of the test-tubes?' Todd asked, studying the dark liquid.

'Todd, do not break one of the tubes.'

Todd's face froze at Hector's no-nonsense tone.

Hawk came strolling up, holding a large key ring with a range of keys. He was grinning. 'That was too easy, the gateman's pretty stupid.'

Hector took the keys. 'See, I told you it's going to work out well,' he told Jamie. He patted Hawk on the back. 'Nice work.'

By now, the road crew had raised many cobbles and Swiper, Zad and Henry were knee-deep in a hole, shovelling earth.

'Dat's grand, lads,' said Hector before whispering, 'Not too fast, lads. Go down about another foot, then place the fake pipe in position.'

Jamie peered over the side of the cart. The yard was bathed in moonlight. The cobbled yard and slate roofs of buildings on the other side of the Thames reflected the silvery rays. The stables were quiet, as was the building above them.

For the moment, they appeared to be alone.

Jamie's gaze fell upon Hector, standing with the gang, sizing up the big hall.

'Here's my chance, lads, we'll be out of here in no time at all,' Hector said, then set off at a sprint.

He opened the small integrated door, releasing a blaze of light and momentarily illuminating part of the yard.

Todd drank from the canteen and screwed the top back on. 'I need to go to the toilet.'

Jamie sighed. 'Oh no, not now. Where are you going to go?'

'I only want to do a whiz. I must have drank a gallon of water today.'

'Can't you wait?'

'I'm busting.'

Jamie lifted the blanket. 'Go over there, by the gates.'

Todd scrambled out of the cart and made for the gates.

When Todd came back to the cart, he was about to climb back on when a voice stopped him dead.

'Where's your foreman?'

Jamie saw Cornelius striding across the yard with Patterson. Was Todd about to be discovered?

Henry's reply was calm. 'Don't know, he was 'ere a minute ago.'

Jamie inched up the blanket in time to see Hector silhouetted leaving the hall in the glare of the gas lamps inside.

'What the... ?' The Dutchman marched up to him, leaving everyone staring in his wake. 'What the hell were you doing in there?'

Todd took his opportunity of boarding the cart. 'That was close,' he whispered, pulling the blanket over him.

'Shhh, Hector's been caught,' Jamie said, peering over the side panels.

The three men stood in the light. Hector pointed and said, 'What de devil is dat t'ing, in der? Oi've never seen its loike before.'

'Never you mind. Tell me what you were doing in there,' Cornelius demanded.

'Oi was only checking if der was a gas main junction point in der. When Oi saw dat arch ting Oi... well, Oi didn't know what to t'ink.'

Cornelius's reply was abrupt. 'There will not be *any* work carried out in there tonight. Do you understand? Maybe tomorrow. This hall is definitely out of bounds. I'm sure this door was locked.' He closed it firmly and locked it. 'I need to know how long you and your men are going to be. There's going to be a lot of activity here, soon.'

'Oi can't put a time on it, sir, dese t'ings take as long as dey take.'

Cornelius and Patterson accompanied Hector over to the gang, who were thigh-deep in a trench, standing either side of the dummy black pipe they had fixed in place.

'Well done, lads. Have you found any leaks?' Henry said they hadn't. 'We will have to follow dis pipe along de yard until we find de leak. We'll refill as we go.'

Cornelius signalled to Patterson and turned his back on them and walked angrily away.

'Well, did you get what you wanted?' Henry asked.

Hector handed the keys to Hawk. 'Here, go and return these. Put them on the floor or something, I'll leave it up to you.' He walked over to the cart and lifted the blanket. 'It's not good news, I'm afraid. The crystal wasn't there. Things are definitely *not* cool.'

'Oh, no,' Jamie said. 'What now?'

Hector pulled out his watch. 'It's half past nine. We have no choice but to wait for the army to arrive, then somehow make for the crystal.'

'But when the army come and are sent back in time, it's game over, isn't it?' Todd asked.

'What's 'appening, 'ector?' Henry interrupted, leaning on his shovel. 'Did you get what you wanted?'

Hector walked slowly back to the gang. 'No, I didn't.'

'So what now?' Swiper enquired.

Hector turned away and took several deliberate steps. 'I didn't think this would happen, we should be making our getaway now.'

J.T. threw down his shovel. 'So how long you wanting us to stay 'ere? 'Cause we've done our part of the deal, we 'elped you get in.'

'I paid you to help me get out, as well.'

'*So what* is it you want, anyway?' Zad asked, his glistening bald head mirroring the moon's rays.

'It must be worff a lot, if he's paying us £100,' said Philip, rubbing his head through the bandana.

'Maybe 'e should pay us more, then,' came J.T.'s grumpy suggestion.

Hector sighed. 'Henry, I paid you in good faith to help see me through the job. And you agreed.' He stared fixedly at the leader.

Henry hesitated. Doubt crept across his features. 'I did, but 'ow long do we 'ave to stay 'ere?'

'I really don't know!' Hector's voice rose with each word. Squabbling and bickering broke out, then laughter.

The wrangling faded, leaving J.T. rumbling with mirth.

'What's so funny?' Hector snapped.

'You,' replied J.T. 'You look ridiculous in that beard. Looks like you're being attacked by a fox!'

The Holton gang stared up at Hector. Henry began to laugh, setting off the others. Hector's shoulders started to shake until he, too, joined in the laughter. 'All right,' he said. 'Another £50, but you must stay with me.'

Henry broke into a broad, delighted grin. 'Very well, 'ector, £50 it is.'

Hector reached for a shovel and handed it to Swiper. 'I'll pay you when we leave here. Now take the pipe out and fill the hole, then dig a little further.'

'You can do a bit of digging now, don't be coy,' said J.T.

'I'm the foreman,' said Hector. 'Besides, I'm paying you lot a fortune.'

'What's Hector playing at?' Todd asked, under the blanket. 'When the soldiers turn up the whole world's done for, isn't it?'

Jamie's sigh was long as he closed his eyes. Surely his hope of returning home was not to be dashed again. Not now, with Todd's deadly predicament making their situation even more formidable.

The sound of scraping in the distance disturbed his thoughts. Now a constant grating noise, it grew louder by the second.

'What's that?' Todd asked.

'It's the army, it's got to be.'

The sound of the gates opening had Todd fretting. 'You're right, it *is* the army. What can Hector do? How is he going to get the crystal with 3000 soldiers here?' He flinched, holding his stomach. 'Cramp,' he moaned.

Not now! thought Jamie.

Jamie pushed up the blanket enough to see a column of soldiers marching, flanked by officers on horseback. The slow-moving army began to pass and as Jamie watched, an officer on horseback ambled towards the cart. Jamie slowly let the blanket down, sensing that the officer was inspecting the cart. He nudged Todd and told him to keep quiet.

'Can Oi help you, sir?' Hector asked.

'What's going on, here?' enquired the officer.

'Der's a gas leak, but we hope to find it soon.'

'Hmm, that's a spot of bad luck. Very good, carry on.'

J.T. rested his shovel on his shoulder. 'I'm ex-army but those uniforms are from an age gone by.' He shook his head and spat, 'They're from the 1700s!' His tone changed to one of wonder. 'But their rifles... they're right up to date.'

'What the 'ell is 'appening, 'ector?' Henry wanted to know.

Jamie observed the soldiers, dressed as 18th-Century infantrymen, filling the yard, but he didn't know how a soldier of the day would look.

'It must be some kind of military exercise, I don't know,' Hector replied.

The soldiers wore long red coats and black tri-cornered hats. Agents positioned them into columns in the yard. The white bands across their chests were clearly visible.

'What's happening now?' Todd asked, clutching his stomach.

'I can see Cornelius; he's joking with an army officer. Now the huge wooden doors are opening.' He whistled softly when the light from the hall fell on the army occupying the yard. 'There's so many soldiers. Cornelius is now standing between the open doors with Patterson and the army officer. That old scientist is pointing towards the arch.'

The officer rapped out an order and the army turned to face the hall. Another order commanded three rows of soldiers into the hall. When enough soldiers were in the hall, agents closed the big wooden doors.

Henry looked up at Hector who stood like stone, intently watching the closing doors. 'Hey, 'ector, 'ow you gonna get what you want wiv all those soldiers in there?'

'My chance will come, you'll see,' Hector said.

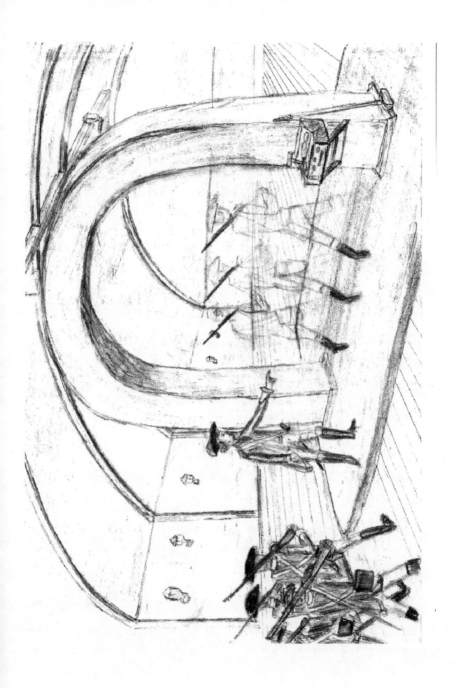

***

The military operation continued. It was 11 o'clock and, although all was not lost, with the tail-end of the regiment about to enter the hall, Hector paced anxiously, cracking his knuckles.

He had told Todd to keep drinking the water; for the moment, it was keeping the cholera at bay. Todd, knowing only that his thirst was fierce, obeyed.

From the cart, Jamie gazed up at the moon behind hazy clouds; the night had steadily grown colder and it was as if the moon was frozen in the night sky. And it had changed position, noticeably; evidence that time was moving on. 'It rotates at the same time as it revolves round the Earth. That's why we always see the same face. Amazing, eh?'

'What?' Todd asked.

'The moon, it rotates at the same – '

'Jamie, this isn't the *time,* or the *place* for space facts.'

Jamie agreed, but he was trying to take his mind from the desperate situation, and Hector's tense mood didn't help.

Henry and his gang stood idly in and around the ditch. They had stopped digging some time ago. The gang-leader laughed with bewilderment and said, 'Tell me, 'ector, where 'ave all them soldiers gone? I just don't know what's goin' on.'

'Don't worry, Henry. The time is close at hand – '

The big doors opened again. When the interior lights illuminated the remaining army, the order was given to enter.

Hector called to Jamie and Todd. 'You two might as well get off the cart and brace yourselves; things are going to get a little lively soon.'

Climbing off the cart, Jamie found that his legs and feet were numb with the cold.

Todd took another swig from the canteen.

Hector retrieved a tube fixed to a tripod from the cart. 'When this goes off, it's going to fill the whole area with smoke. Now Jamie, when it starts to smoke, I want you to send the first explosive test-tube onto the roof of the hall, then continue at random, make it seem that the whole place is under attack. And Todd, stay with him always, never leave his side, and be ready with the test-tubes.' Todd nodded. Hector glanced across the yard at a column of soldiers pushing hand-carts into the hall. 'That's the rounds of ammunition going in. Not long now.'

Hector approached the Holton gang. 'We'll soon be leaving here, but first, I need your help.' He placed the tripod on the ground and spoke to Henry. 'I want you,

J.T., Zad and Philip to come with me into the hall; I feel there's going to be fisticuffs.'

Henry took a deep breath. 'We're ready.'

Hector spoke to Hawk. 'When we enter the hall, go with Swiper and use the chloroform on the gateman and tie him up. Then open the gates and wait on the cart for us.'

Hector attended to the tripod. Jamie noticed Todd looking apprehensive. Was he going to have another attack of cramp?

Hector lit the fuse and it sparked into life, fizzing towards the tube. 'We've got two or three minutes before that starts to smoke,' he told Henry, and led the gang-leader and his friends to the hall.

Seeing Hawk and Swiper walking towards the gatehouse raised Jamie's pulse even more.

'I don't know what Hector's playing at,' said Todd, watching the fuse burn. 'If he does get the crystal, so what? The damage would already have been done.'

'He must know what he's doing. Well, I hope he knows what he's doing.' Jamie stared intently at the burning fuse. He held back the elastic of the catapult. When the fuse reached the tube and nothing happened, he cursed. 'I knew it! It's another thing he's put together that hasn't worked.'

'Just start the attack in a minute or two,' said Todd.

Jamie shook his head, 'We can't. If I did that, we'd all be sitting ducks.'

Jamie was suddenly grabbed roughly around the midriff, causing him to drop the test-tube! He knew all too well not to step on the explosive fluid, but where *was* it?

XVIII

Jamie tried desperately to keep his feet still. One wrong move and who knew what harm the blast would do?

'What are you doing here?' demanded one of the agents. 'I was with Cornelius today at the hotel when he retrieved the crystal. I don't know what's going on but I'm taking you to Corn – '

The agent received a heavy blow to the back of his head from Hawk. Immediately, Jamie felt the man's grip loosen, then saw him collapse to the ground.

The explosives! 'Stand back, Hawk!' Jamie shouted, crouching low.

'What you doing?' Hawk asked.

Jamie patted the ground frantically, amazed the tube hadn't been trodden on. Todd came over with one

280

of the lamps, enabling Jamie to spot the test-tube and retrieve it.

Hawk and Swiper were dragging the agent to the gatehouse as Todd reminded Jamie about the smoke-screen not working.

'Hector must be wondering why the stun bombs haven't gone off,' Jamie said, holding the catapult ready for the bombardment. He stomped towards the tripod and kicked it. 'Start, you bastard!' The sudden jolt must have got it working; thick black smoke began pouring out. Within moments the billowing clouds filled the yard.

'Nice one, Jamie!' Todd said, raising his fist.

Then, engulfed in smoke, Jamie heard him groan. 'Todd, you all right?' he asked.

Todd, crouching, struggled to answer. 'N... n... no, I'm not.'

'Drink more water.'

Todd gulped some down as Jamie sent a test-tube high up into the night sky in the direction of the hall. It landed on the roof, instantly followed by a stomach-churning explosion. Todd fought to stand as he passed Jamie another test-tube. This time, Jamie targeted the water's edge, and with success - a similar, deafening bang ensued.

Jamie ran to the huge doors to the hall. Peering through a gap, he could see that Hector had ensnared Cornelius and Patterson in netting. Close by, Zad held an agent above his head and then, with arms outstretched, flung the man to the floorboards, winding him. Philip and J.T. wrestled with two agents whilst Henry roamed the hall like a man possessed. He was dispatching Cornelius's men with his bare hands, one after the other.

Hector ran to the arch. As he approached it, Jamie saw five soldiers materialise at the far end of the hall. 'Look! The soldiers are returning!' he cried.

'Fire one - ' Todd stopped to breathe deeply. 'Fire one in the hall!' Todd tried to push open one of the huge doors, but his strength was draining away.

The smoke-screen reached the hall, shrouding them in clouds of black smoke.

'Give me the test-tubes,' Jamie ordered Todd, 'and go and wait on the cart.' He collected the last three tubes and lined them up in his back pocket.

As Todd left for the cart, Jamie barged the doors open. Soldiers were now appearing all over the hall. Jamie let a test-tube fly. It sailed through the air until it hit the floor close to a group of soldiers. They scattered immediately. He fired another at another gathering of troops with the same devastating effect.

Hector, Henry and his boys ran to leave the hall, while Cornelius threw the netting off, shouting to Hector to stop. Hector was first to disappear into the heavy cloud of black smoke. The race was on for the cart, which was now positioned between the open gates.

Jamie joined Henry and his gang, running blindly through the smoke-screen, as a gun-shot rang out, followed by another.

Jamie unleashed the final test-tube in the direction of the pursuing soldiers charging from behind him. Yet another explosion followed. He scrambled onto the cart, and watched Hector and Henry close the gates.

As soon as the gates slammed together, a barrage of rifle-fire peppered them.

Swiper cracked the whip and the big shire horse broke into a lumbering trot.

'We have to *rendezvous* with Catherine, remember?' Hector told Swiper, then paused, straining to listen. He turned to Jamie. 'Police whistles. I thought they would come eventually.'

The gang was in too high spirits to care. 'Them explosions was incredible! 'Arf of London must 'ave 'eard 'em.' Henry chuckled and clapped his hands.

Hawk chipped in, 'And your smoke fing didn't work at first, Jamie 'ad to kick it over to get it working.'

'I did wonder why it took so long,' said Hector. 'And by the way, you fought like tigers back there; those agents never got the chance to draw their pistols. I think you would make fine soldiers and I would be proud to serve with you. Have any of you considered a career in the army?'

But his question fell on deaf ears; the gang was too busy laughing and joking.

Hector stared at Todd, slouched at the back of the cart. 'How are you, Todd?'

Todd clutched his stomach. 'The pain's came back... worse.'

Hector gave a sympathetic smile. 'Not long now. You both did really well.'

Jamie took the praise with mixed feelings; the police whistles in the distance were definitely growing louder.

'Don't worry,' Hector said, showing them the crystal. 'We'll soon be away from here.'

Jamie was confused. 'I don't get it. The army was sent back in time, but the world seems all right to me. Nothing's changed.'

Hector smiled. 'On the contrary. Before I left the hall the first time, I was able to alter the mechanisms. When the arch was activated, the soldiers were sent 90 minutes into the *future*. Although I should have sent them further, I couldn't believe it when they started to reappear. I didn't want to tell you at the time, because I wasn't sure it was going to work.'

'So what happened in the hall?'

'When I entered the hall, I saw Cornelius arguing with Albert. Cornelius had the history book open and was looking at the pages, demanding to know why history hadn't altered. When Cornelius and Patterson saw me without the false beard, they were very taken aback! When they asked what I was doing there, and I told them I had come back from the dead, you should have seen their faces. They looked as if they'd seen a ghost.'

Jamie laughed.

'So, 'ector,' Henry called, 'Did you get what you wanted?'

Hector nodded triumphantly. 'I certainly did.'

The gang-leader held out his hand. 'I fink you owe us somefing.'

Hector smiled. 'So what are you going to do with all the money?' he asked, reaching for his wallet.

Henry shrugged. 'We'll fink of somefing.'

Swiper pulled the cart to a stop, alongside an anxious Catherine, who was standing in front of the parked carriage. 'Is everything all right? I heard the explosions, they were so loud,' she said.

'Everything's splendid,' Hector told her. He offered his hand to the gang-leader. 'Well, so long, Henry, it's been a pleasure to know you. All of you for that matter; I'm grateful to all of you and would never have succeeded without your help.'

Henry shook his hand. 'If ever you're passing, just call in, but you better do it soon, we'll be moving out before long.'

Jamie felt sorry to see the gang go. He would miss them.

Catherine rushed to Hector and threw her arms around him. 'I was so worried when the explosions were going off. Do you have the crystal?'

Hector nodded.

'That's great news,' said Catherine. She noticed Todd still lying in the cart. 'Are you all right, Todd?'

'He will be, as soon as they're back where they belong,' said Hector. He held Catherine's hand with obvious excitement. 'We could go with them, you know.'

Catherine took a deep breath. 'Hector Edward Lightfoot, you know my feelings regarding time-travel and *still* you try to change my mind. So you don't want to marry me, is that it?'

'Soaring eagles!' Hector exclaimed, dropping to one knee. 'Of course I want to marry you.' He looked up at her and asked, 'Catherine Wallace, will you marry me, in *this* time, and make me the happiest man alive?'

'Yes, yes, but on one condition.'

'Name it.'

'That you get your hair cut.'

'I'll go to the barber-shop, tomorrow.'

Hector looked at his watch. 'Just 22 minutes to go,' he said, serious once more. 'Don't worry, we have plenty of time to get to Bedford Square, so you can settle in the house.' The sound of galloping hooves attracted his attention. 'It can't be the police already,' he said, squinting down the street.

A lone horseman came charging round the bend of Lower Thames Street towards them.

'It's Cornelius!' Hector cried. 'He must have taken a horse from the stables. Quickly, inside the carriage, I do believe things are going to turn nasty.'

XIX

Jamie's legs almost buckled as he climbed on to the footstep to help Todd into the carriage. As his friend groaned and clutched his stomach, Jamie feared that his illness was about to get much worse. Hector was already up in the driver's seat and, as soon as the door banged shut, he cracked the whip with a commanding shout, causing the horses to bolt.

The carriage accelerated, but Cornelius was rapidly closing on them. Jamie watched him draw level. Hector swerved into him, but Cornelius was a skilful horseman and avoided a collision. Once more he drew level , gun in hand.

Todd clutched his stomach again. The empty canteen dropped to the floor.

As the gun went off, a flash discharged from the nozzle, making Jamie and Catherine jump. 'I hope that missed Hector,' he said, gripping the handrails.

Catherine was now at the window. Her face was pale. 'Good heavens above, I can't bear this. How long can Hector avoid being hit?'

Suddenly, the carriage braked, throwing Jamie and Catherine forward; then a sharp left turn sent them stumbling to the window. As Hector pushed the horses on, Cornelius fired again.

'Jamie, use your sling-shot!' Catherine cried.

Jamie grabbed Todd's arm. 'Give me some stones.'

Todd's face twisted with pain. 'I haven't got any left.'

Buildings flashed by. The carriage swerved again, causing Cornelius to fall back. But he soon came charging up on the other side. Jamie caught sight of St Paul's Cathedral ahead. The white stonework reflected the moon's rays, but the dome was a mere silhouette against the black sky.

Another shot rang out and the carriage reduced speed.

'Something's happened,' Catherine cried. 'The carriage is deviating. Oh my God, Hector's been hit!'

Something *was* wrong. Jamie saw Cornelius raise his arm to shoot again as the carriage slowed down, but when he pulled the trigger there was no discharge.

'He's run out of bullets!' Jamie shouted.

Cornelius threw the weapon down and slipped his feet from the stirrups, all the while nudging closer to the carriage.

Catherine stared wildly at Jamie. 'He's going to board the coach!'

Climbing up onto to the saddle, Cornelius steadied himself briefly before jumping on to the roof and landing with a loud thud. Hector gave a banshee-like cry and cracked the whip, sending the horses into a gallop once again. They heard another thud, which they knew must be Cornelius crashing to the roof. Then, from above, came sounds of a frantic tussle. The carriage was now driverless! It rocked violently from side to side, threatening to overturn at any moment.

Catherine clasped her head as Jamie opened the carriage door. He was reaching for the handrails on the roof, and using the seat to hoist himself up. 'What are you doing, Jamie? Get back inside!' she screamed.

Jamie ignored her and hauled himself up the side-panelling. Temple Bar lay ahead. The ancient white stone gateway almost glowed in the moonlight. The driverless carriage was rapidly approaching it.

With the ground passing at a dizzying speed below, Jamie peered over the roof and gasped; Cornelius was squeezing Hector's throat and Hector could only hold on to Cornelius's arms.

'I'm going to finish you off once and for all, and rule the world!' Cornelius snarled.

Jamie looked on helplessly. Hector was losing the fight!

Building after building flashed by. Hurtling along Fleet Street, all Jamie could do was hold on tightly while watching the struggle. 'What's happening up there?' Catherine cried.

Somehow, Hector brought his feet to Cornelius's stomach, and then thrust his legs out in a desperate effort to pitch the madman from the roof. But Cornelius held on and scrambled to his feet, balancing with agility. Hector, exhausted, offered no resistance.

Cornelius produced a knife from inside his coat. 'No!' Jamie screamed, grabbing Cornelius's ankle.

Jamie's desperate action startled Cornelius, though only briefly. He gazed down at Jamie's head and grinned triumphantly.

As the speeding coach raced past Chancery Lane and through Temple Bar, there came a sudden sickening thud. Cornelius had smashed into the stone arch. Jamie looked back at the road to see his arch enemy sprawled out under the arch. 'He's gone! Cornelius is gone!' he shouted.

Catherine leant outside the carriage. 'But what about Hector? Is he all right?'

Jamie was too occupied to answer. He'd seen Hector slump into the driver's seat, but when the carriage failed to slow down, he hurled himself onto the front of the vehicle. There, he found Hector slouched in the seat and clutching his shoulder.

'Hector, what's wrong?' Jamie lurched next to him on to the seat.

Hector's face contorted with pain. 'I'm sorry, Jamie, but I can't retrieve the reins.'

'Don't worry, I'll get them.'

'No, Jamie, it's too dangerous.'

But Jamie was already kneeling, searching for the reins. He soon found them, dangling on one of the shafts. He edged forwards, conscious that his head was only inches from one horse's hindquarters. He leaned on the shaft, and clutching wildly at the elusive reins with his fingertips again and again, but he couldn't reach.

'Soaring eagles, be careful, Jamie!' Hector howled.

Jamie crawled further along the shaft, until his whole body was balanced on it precariously.

At last, his fingers clasped the reins. But returning to the carriage proved even more hazardous. He wobbled on the vibrating shaft. With the reins still in his hands, Jamie slipped, his foot scraping the cobbles of The Strand. In one concentrated bout of effort, he inched back to safety, and passed the reins over to Hector.

After a short struggle, Hector eventually brought the horses to a stop, no more than 50 yards from Trafalgar Square.

The engineer inhaled deeply. The coach door opened. 'Oh Hector, are you all right?' Catherine cried. 'Good heavens above, what's happened here?'

'Young Jamie retrieved the reins,' replied Hector. 'If it wasn't for him, Lord knows what would have happened.' He raised his arm, feebly, pointing. 'We'd probably be sitting up there with Nelson, on top of his column.'

It was then that he noticed Jamie rubbing his right hand. 'What have you done, Jamie?'

'When I slipped, I landed awkwardly on my hand.'

'Let me see,' said Catherine, gently taking his wrist. 'Can you move your fingers?'

Jamie winced but succeeded in bending them.

'I don't think it's broken, but there is some swelling.'

Hector laughed weakly. 'We're the walking wounded.'

He flinched with pain and Catherine hurried to attend to him. 'I can see blood,' she gasped, 'and there's a hole in your coat. Hector, you've been shot, oh my God, I knew it. You've been shot.'

Hector winced. 'I need the bullet removed from my shoulder, but first we must deliver these boys back to the house.' He pulled out his watch. 'We have just a little over 13 minutes to midnight.' He paused for breath. 'The horses need attention, Catherine. Put the blankets over them, we'll give them water as soon as we can find a trough.'

Catherine saw to the horses and then drove through the narrow back streets, stopping close to Bedford Square. She joined Hector and the boys inside the carriage.

Hector clutched his shoulder. 'Are you sure you don't mind being left here?' he asked. 'The house is only a short walk.'

'Of course not,' said Jamie. 'But I'm worried about Todd.'

Hector focused on Todd, whose pale face and darkened eyes were evident in the darkness. 'As soon as you get back to the house, drink plenty of water, you must be dehydrating again. And once back in your time, see a doctor *immediately*. I'm sure everything will end favourably.'

'And *you* must get to a doctor, quickly,' Jamie said.

Hector smiled. 'They're a couple of exceptional boys,' he told Catherine.

'They certainly are; I think the future's safe with young people like them.'

Hector nodded, then flinched in pain again.

'This must be like the time you last got shot, fighting the Afghans,' Jamie observed.

Hector nodded. 'Yes, but not as bad, thank heavens.'

For a moment they were silent; the time had come to say farewell forever. It was Hector who spoke first. 'I've enjoyed meeting you, Jamie, Todd. If it wasn't for you, I'd still be in hiding, but now I have my freedom, *and* I'm marrying a wonderful lady.'

Catherine smiled. 'You'll be able to help your friend now. The Colonel.'

Hector smiled. 'Yes, poor Godfrey. That will be my priority.'

'It's been good knowing you two, as well,' Jamie said. 'I'll never forget you.'

'Or me,' Todd blurted.

'Would you mind if I gave them this watch?' Hector asked Catherine.

'Of course not. I can get you another.'

Hector handed Jamie the watch. 'A memento from the 19th Century.'

'Thanks,' Jamie said. 'I meant to ask you. What will happen to that man, Travis? The one who was sent back in time.'

'He will just have to remain in the 18th Century and will soon realise that something went wrong.' He gave instructions as to what they must do at the house and nodded to the door. 'Go on, it's almost time.' He shook the boys' hands, but Jamie had to use his left; the pain in his right was worsening.

'Off you go, now,' Hector said.

Catherine frowned. 'Hector, have you given them the crystal?' she asked.

'Soaring eagles!' Hector exclaimed, 'I haven't!' He brought it out. 'Now that would have been a disaster.'

Taking it, Jamie saw the funny side. He laughed.

Catherine took the reins, with Hector sitting by her side. 'Well, goodbye boys,' said the engineer, looking down at them standing in the road. 'Good luck, and have a good life.'

Jamie and Todd waved them off and Catherine gently pulled away. They stood watching, as the horses moved into a trot.

'I'm really going to miss them,' Jamie said, straining for a last glimpse of the carriage.

'Me too,' Todd replied, rubbing his stomach. 'And in a way, I'm going to miss this time, as well.'

'I'll see if I do when we get back,' Jamie said.

Todd hesitated. 'I'm a bit worried, the way Hector said I must see a doctor. What's wrong? What have I got?'

Jamie didn't answer, he just shrugged.

Todd looked squarely at Jamie but nothing else was said.

Bathed in moonlight, Bedford Square looked tranquil as ever. The silence was broken only by their footsteps. They passed a horseless wagon, no other vehicle was in the square.

Jamie pulled the planks away from the damaged door of the house with his good hand, while Todd checked the area. As Jamie yanked off the last piece of wood, the door slowly opened. As it did so, a loud whistle-blast sounded nearby. The boys gasped as uniformed police appeared. They came charging from the gardens opposite the house and from the parked wagon. With no time to escape, Jamie and Todd found themselves confronted by a sergeant and 10 stern-looking constables.

XX

'Trying to burgle this house, eh?' the sergeant accused. He turned to one of his constables. 'It's fortunate that I heard this house was broken into last night. I told you they'd be back tonight.'

'You're a very astute man, Sidney,' his colleague observed.

'I like to think so.'

'You're making a big mistake,' said Jamie.

Sidney sighed and rolled his eyes, 'Save it for the judge in the morning.'

Jamie's legs weakened. Was this how it would end - with them both heading for the dock in the morning and no Hector coming to their rescue? But as he and Todd edged towards the officers, Jamie spied a gap in their ranks. If they could make their escape... in one swift movement, he pulled Todd by the arm. 'Run for it, Todd!' he shouted.

'After them!' bellowed the sergeant. 'I want two men stationed here.' Officers sprang into action on his command. To a shrill chorus of police whistles, Jamie and Todd sprinted free of the square, into Gower Street. Todd held his stomach as he ran.

'What do we do now?' Todd panted, when they were clear.

'We've got to get back to the square. I know you're ill, Todd, but you've got to lead the way, so I'm relying on you.' Jamie panted, then nodded, 'Go for it!'

Todd took a left turn.

The haunting wail of the police whistles gave the impression that the constabulary had besieged the whole of Bloomsbury.

As they sprinted along the street, exhaling clouds of frozen breath, Todd constantly turned to look over his shoulder. 'We're done for,' he said, panting.

As they approached Tottenham Court Road, the sound of running footsteps made them dive low beside the wall of a corner house. Jamie crouched, gasping at the coldness of the ground, as four officers ran past just yards away. He shuddered at the thought of running straight into their arresting hands.

Todd groaned and curled over. 'Cramp,' he gasped. 'It's... really bad, this time.'

Jamie stared at Todd. Not now! Todd was keeling over, gurgling, both hands massaging his stomach.

Jamie hesitated. 'Todd, we must get going. Can you still run?'

Todd tried to get up and moaned. 'I don't think I can. Ah!' he cried. 'What's wrong with me? I think I've got something bad.'

Jamie took a quick glance over his shoulder, listening to the police whistles. If the police were to appear, they would be done for. He dropped to one knee. Not only were they not going to make it home, Todd could die.

'Sorry, Jamie. Why don't you try and make it?'

Jamie shook his head with eyes closed. 'No way, Todd. I would never leave you here.' Jamie couldn't believe Todd was thinking of him. He knew Todd had to see a doctor, but first they had to get off the street. 'We'll hide behind this wall. Don't worry Todd, we'll find a doctor somehow.'

Todd got to his feet, grizzling. 'The cramp's eased a little.'

'Do you think you can go on?'

Wincing, Todd nodded.

'Great! We've got one advantage,' said Jamie. 'They won't be expecting us to double-back.'

'But they've got two coppers outside the house. How are we going to get in there?'

'Let's just get to the square first.' Jamie glanced at the watch and gasped. 'We've got four minutes.'

They set off, with Todd clutching his stomach and Jamie fearing the worst.

Having gone full circle, they crept along the street which led back to the square. Stopping on the corner, Jamie pointed to the oval gardens. 'If we can get into there, it'll give us good cover to get close to the house.'

Quietly, they scuttled across the cobbled street to the iron railings.

Jamie knelt on all fours so Todd could use him as a step.

'What's wrong?' Todd whispered, standing on the other side of the railings.

'It's my hand; it hurts too much to take my weight.'

Todd slipped his arms though the railings, cupping his hands to make a step for him.

'Are you sure you've got the strength to take my weight?'

'Just do it, will you,' snapped Todd.

Jamie put his foot on the makeshift step and scrambled over the barrier.

A grimacing Todd rubbed his arms.

'Is it cramp again?'

'Yeah, but I'm OK.'

Using the undergrowth as cover, they hurried past the trees to stand at the main entrance, and stood gazing at the house; their gateway to their own time was guarded by two caped policemen.

'We're finished,' said Todd, shaking his head. 'We don't even know where to find Hector and Catherine. I suppose we could always rejoin Henry's gang.'

Jamie bit his lip. If Todd knew he had cholera, then he would have something else to worry about. 'There must be a way of getting in there,' he said under his breath.

Todd flinched with pain again, gripping his stomach. 'What do you suggest, we go over there... and beat them up?' he struggled to say.

Jamie contemplated bursting through the gates using the catapult for a shoot-out but they only had one chance. Besides, Todd could have a severe bout of cramp and collapse. Jamie stared at the ground, defeated. A smooth, round stone reflecting the moonlight caught his eye. 'We're not finished yet,' he said, whipping out the catapult. 'If I can break a window it will draw the coppers away.' He winced as he pulled the elastic back. 'Here, take it.' Todd stepped back when Jamie handed him the catapult. 'I can't fire it because of my hand... so you'll have to do it.'

'Me!' Todd exclaimed in a strained whisper. 'I'm cramping up every few seconds.'

'There can't be much more than a minute left. *Do it, Todd.*' Eyeing a row of houses on the far side of the square, Jamie said, 'Hit one of those windows over there.'

Todd shook his head. 'No way, Jamie, you know I'm crap with the catapult.'

'Just aim at the windows, will you? I'll stand behind and guide you.'

Todd rose above the railings, flinching with pain. He eyed the houses and stretched the elastic.

'Aim above the windows,' Jamie said, standing behind with his eyes in line with the vee of the catapult. 'Pull back the elastic some more.'

Todd sighed. 'This is ridiculous, I've never hit a thing before and now you're asking me to hit a window at distance. And it's dark.'

Jamie kept his voice calm. 'Pull it back a bit more.' He noticed Todd's hand shaking; this was hopeless. But Hector wouldn't have given up. 'Keep your hand really still and draw back a little further... fire!' he commanded.

Todd released the stone, but heard no sound. 'I've missed.' He turned away despairingly.

But he hadn't missed; at that moment, the silence in the square gave way to the sound of glass breaking.

'Yes!' cried Todd, jumping up and down. 'I did it!' But his joy was short-lived - he grabbed his stomach and fell to his knees. 'Aargh, the pain! It's terrible.'

Jamie looked from Todd to the policemen. They were startled, staring in the direction of the broken window, and now brandishing their truncheons ready for action. 'Why don't they go and inspect the house? Go... go.' Jamie turned back to Todd. 'Todd, you OK?'

Todd stood up, gingerly, in time to see the two officers leave their post to investigate the noise. 'I'm OK, just.' Together they ran through the open gates towards the house, but Todd's scuffling footsteps were heard.

The policemen, nearing the far side of the square, spun round. 'Hey! Stop!' one ordered, and blew his whistle.

Jamie kicked open the door, only to hear the clock's chimes for midnight had already begun. As he fumbled with the crystal in the moonlit back room, another chime rang out. How many of the 12 were left?

The two policemen entered the house. 'We've got them now, there's no escape in here,' one of them yelled. 'You go upstairs and I'll search down here.'

Jamie knew the arresting officer was only seconds away. He pulled out the iron plate, then offered the crystal up to the clock face, and tried to locate the hole.

But it eluded him. Todd grabbed Jamie's injured hand tightly as another stroke of the clock sounded. Standing on the plate with Todd, Jamie stifled a groan as a searing pain almost made him drop the crystal. He gripped it tightly, and finally found the slot. Todd had the trunk door open, and was ready to pull down the regulator.

Suddenly, a policeman appeared at the doorway. 'Pull it, now,' Jamie whispered.

Todd applied downward pressure and Jamie grabbed hold of him, making sure that he didn't fall.

Instantly, they were thrown violently from side to side as air rushed around them from all directions. Jamie held Todd's arm tightly, dreading his friend collapsing, as powerful forces swirled about them.

Through the turbulence, Jamie marvelled at the sequence of night changing to day in a second, again and again and again. And so it continued. They were wildly shaken as Hector briefly appeared, zoomed into view, then disappeared. As daylight filled the room once more, Hector appeared again, though this time carrying Catherine, who was now wearing a white wedding dress.

Then came a blinding flash. Jamie flinched. Todd's eyes were wide open. Jamie felt he was on some kind of fairground ride, watching night and day, night and day, in succession spinning around them. People they'd never seen before appeared in front of them. The light and dark, light and dark cycle continued at accelerating speed until it became a blur, and all the while they were buffeted by unseen forces.

The vortex of turbulence began to subside, and the flashes of light and dark slowed down. The room had changed. Gone was the Victorian décor, now it looked like the office Jamie remembered.

Todd pointed when he saw Jamie's Uncle Simon enter the room. He whizzed into view then out again.

Uncle Simon came into the room again at a much slower pace, then froze completely, the turbulence spent. Jamie still had hold of Todd, he daren't let him go.

'What's happened?' Jamie whispered hoarsely.

'I think Hector's time machine has frozen us in time,' Todd said, wincing.

'We're not going to remain like this, are we? What are we going to do?'

Todd gulped. 'Hector mentioned that we might have a rough ride, but not this.'

Another blinding light had them cowering, but it was only moments before the sequence of night and day returned at a slow pace.

It was whilst the room was filled with daylight that Jamie saw himself enter the room and approach the desk to pick up the big red folder containing Colonel Ramsbottom's journal. They watched Jamie leave the desk and stop to stare at them. Then it went dark again.

'That's incredible,' said Jamie faintly. *'We're* the ghosts I saw.'

Daylight returned once more with the sun shining through the window.

'Amazing,' said Todd. 'It was us you saw, all the time.'

Jamie was still trying to get his head around the paradox. The night and day sequence had stopped. 'What's happened now?' he asked. 'Are we frozen in time again, or not?' He sighed, then smiled. 'I just saw that electric clock on the desk change to 12 noon. Hector said he'd send us to midday.'

'We've made it!' Todd cried.

Jamie left the clock and headed for the kitchen, as Todd sat down at the desk, taking deep breaths.

When Jamie returned with a glass of water for Todd, his friend pointed.

Jamie looked at the space where the grandfather clock once stood. 'Good ol' Hector, his work is now complete.'

Jamie stared out of the window, rubbing his sore hand. 'I can't believe I saw myself!'

Todd finished the glass of water in one gulp and huffed. 'That was well mental.' He got unsteadily to his feet and took hold of Jamie's hand and shook it. 'If it wasn't for you getting the reins of the carriage and guiding me with the catapult, we wouldn't have made it.'

'Will you stop grabbing my hand!' Jamie screeched, but he had to laugh. 'How are you feeling?'

'The pain's still there.'

It was then, in the sunlight, that Jamie could clearly see that Todd's complexion had a blueish tinge to add to his gaunt features. Was this the final stage of cholera?

Jamie looked away. The time had come to tell Todd of his terrible illness, but his friend spoke first. 'The skill you showed with the catapult was... well, it was phenomenal. Wait till I tell Turbo and Steve how good you are. You're a member of The Riverside Posse, already.'

Jamie smiled. 'You know something? I don't think I want to be in the gang any more. I've had my share of crime, and I definitely don't want to steal from Gracie.'

'What about Carter and his bullying?'

Jamie just shrugged.

'If you join the gang, I know for certain he won't start on you any more.'

'I think I can take him on. I gave you a slap didn't I, and you're a good fighter.' Todd raised his eyebrows. 'It's just, since meeting Hector and Catherine and seeing what they achieved, I think I'll say no to the Riverside Posse, work harder at school and achieve something myself.'

Todd looked confused. 'But... I thought you really wanted to be in the gang.'

Jamie shook his head. 'Not any more, Todd. I'm going to become an astronomer, like Catherine.' He clenched his fist. 'And bring on Hawaii!'

Todd put his hand on Jamie's shoulder. 'We can still be friends, can't we?' he asked.

'Of course.' Jamie couldn't bring himself to tell Todd now; he looked so happy. He had to find Simon and convince him about Todd and their time-trek.

'Don't worry about Carter,' Todd assured him. 'I'll tell him to lay off you, or else.'

In the hallway, they found the street door open.

'Why's the door open?' Todd asked.

'Probably because of the hot weather.'

Without warning, Todd doubled over and grabbed his stomach.

Jamie bit his lip. He couldn't delay any longer telling Todd what he knew. He went to close the door, when a noise inside the front room stopped him. 'I hope that's Simon in there,' he whispered.

'Me too,' Todd said, massaging his stomach. 'I hope Hector hasn't sent us too far into the future, and it's the next owner.'

'If it is, we'll be accused of house-breaking again. What shall we do?'

Todd froze. 'Wait a minute. Hector said something about if he sent us back to a day we've already lived, we could bump into ourselves and cause something really bad.'

'So what are you saying, it could be you and me in there?'

Todd nodded.

Jamie thought for a moment, then made for the front room door. 'We have no choice, the time machine's gone.'

He turned the handle. In the office were Simon and two other men wearing suits.

'Jamie!' said Simon, rising to his feet.

'So this is your nephew and his friend, I take it?' asked one of the men.

'Er, yes, Inspector. It appears there's been a big mistake,' Simon replied awkwardly. 'Sorry to have wasted your time.'

The two suited men made for the door, stopping briefly in front of Jamie and Todd. The Inspector studied their tatty clothes. 'You've caused your uncle a lot of stress. Next time, tell him where you're going,' he said.

Simon led the policemen out into the hall.

'He's not going to believe us,' said Jamie.

Simon had returned. 'Let's hear it anyway, because I've been worried sick. I was about to ring your mothers. I really expected better from you, Jamie. And why are you both dressed like tramps - '

'It's not our fault, Simon,' Jamie interrupted. 'We... were sent back in time.'

Simon laughed.

'It's true,' said Todd, sitting down gingerly. 'That arched thing under the museum is a time machine built by Hector Lightfoot. When the museum was hit by lightning, it somehow sent us back in time. We actually met Hector.'

Simon sighed. 'Stop this nonsense and tell me where you've been all night.'

'Please believe us, Simon,' said Jamie. How on earth was he was going to convince Simon about Todd having cholera? 'And we weren't gone for one night; we've been gone for four nights. Hector invented a time machine inside a grandfather clock and put it in the other room. He set it so that only a day has gone by in this time.'

'I can't believe I'm having this conversation,' said Simon. 'So you met Hector, yes?' Simon scanned their faces. 'All right, show me the time machine.'

Jamie's gaze fell to the floor. 'It's gone; Hector set it that way, so no one else could threaten the world again.'

Todd yelped suddenly and curled over, clutching his stomach.

'Todd's got cholera!' Jamie exclaimed. 'Hector told me. Can't you see? *Look at his face!*'

'What?' Simon sounded incredulous.

Jamie fished out the watch and held it by its gold chain for Simon to take. 'Here, take a look at this. Hector gave it to me.'

Simon inspected the watch closely, his eyes widening when he looked at the back. He gently put down the mobile phone he was holding. 'I don't believe it.' Simon read aloud. *'To my dearest Hector, hold on to this time and not the future. Much love, Catherine.* I just don't believe it.' Then he snapped into action, snatching up his mobile phone. 'We need an ambulance, right now.'

Jamie sighed. At last. Simon believed him!

Simon had reached the emergency services; he gave his address.

As he clicked off his mobile, Todd began to groan, his face warped with pain.

Pouring water from a bottle into a glass, Simon passed it to Todd. 'Don't worry, Todd, I'm sure they can cure cholera swiftly these days. God knows what explanation we can give for how you got it, though.' Simon turned to Jamie. 'I don't know how it came about, it possibly came from one of the other scientists, but an account of the time-travel project was discovered in the lab. Obviously, we thought it was an elaborate hoax. And the reason I know this is not a wind-up, is because how could you possibly know about Catherine's constant disapproval of Hector's quest for time-travel? The account mentioned something about it going against her morals, although she did assist him earlier on.'

'That's right,' said Jamie. 'She told us that.'

Simon snorted with disbelief then looked at Todd's bruised eye. 'How did he get the shiner?'

'He had a couple of fights.'

Simon shook his head slowly. 'I can't believe what you've experienced. It should have been me! I'm the historian. When you get better, Todd, I want you and Jamie to take me to all the places you visited and tell me the whole story as you go. And I want to know *everything.*

'That was quick,' he said, spotting the ambulance outside. 'It must have been in the locality already.'

Jamie went out to meet the paramedics. As he stepped outside, a scream from inside the house prompted him to rush back in. Todd lay on the floor in the hallway, crying out in pain.

'He just collapsed,' Simon said.

Jamie stepped back and allowed the paramedics to lay their stretcher on the floor. He felt Simon's hand on his shoulder. 'You better get checked out yourself, Jamie; in case you have it as well.'

Epilogue

It was break time at Broomhall High. A faint moon hung high in an all-blue sky, like a perfect circular cloud.

Jamie waited outside the entrance, opposite the playing fields where a noisy, impromptu, five-a-side football match was taking place. Turbo, Steve and Wayne Carter were there, as was Javheed, who minded one of the goals. But no Todd.

Pulling up his sleeve, he checked his Hawaiian tan once more. It was still there, but not as deep as when he had returned a week ago. He thought of the time he had spent up Mount Mauna Kea looking at the skies through the big telescopes. The experience had strengthened his resolve to become an astronomer. The Deputy Head had even let him drop Art so he could have extra Science lessons, where the teacher would let him study astronomy.

He looked up at the moon, thinking of how he had seen it over 100 years earlier. The heavenly body had become like a reliable companion, making him feel safe whenever he saw it.

The entrance doors swung open and Todd stepped out with a teacher, Mr Stark.

'I'm serious, Todd,' the teacher said. 'That essay you presented about Hector Lightfoot was... great, I'm not exaggerating here. Though the grammar could do with a little polishing.'

Todd rolled his eyes at Jamie. 'You're embarrassing me, Mr Stark.'

'Sir,' Jamie nodded a greeting to the science teacher.

Stark pointed at Jamie, 'I expected *his* work to be good, but yours, it was a real eye-opener. I loved the concept you used; going back in time and meeting the engineer. It seemed so... real.'

Jamie glanced at Todd, hiding a smile.

'Have you ever thought of taking up creative writing?' Mr Stark asked.

Todd shrugged. 'Not really.'

'Well, you should. I'm putting your essay up for a special award – '

'Oh, sir,' Todd looked across to his mates playing football. 'You don't have to do that.'

Mr Stark shook his head and said, 'Don't waste that talent, Todd.' He then marched off.

Todd nodded towards the football game. 'Why aren't you playing?'

'I thought I'd wait for you.'

Todd sighed. 'You haven't got to wait for me.'

'I know.' As they started a slow walk towards the game, Jamie asked, 'So will you be taking up writing?'

Todd laughed. 'I don't know. I just want to tell people what happened to us. I would love to tell Mr Stark, he'd be – '

'No, Todd. Never tell anyone. Only my uncle must ever know. The men in white coats would come for you, if you started spouting off.'

'But it was a massive thing that happened, Jamie, I very nearly died!'

'I *know,*' Jamie said. 'You got away with it when you told the doctors; they just thought you were delirious.'

Todd looked bewildered. 'All the stuff that happened is doing my head in. I still can't believe that you and me was the two ghosts the police chased into the house, the same ghosts you saw. And what about The Grand Plan, what would have happened if that had succeeded?'

'But it didn't, did it?' Jamie said.

'You're a real true friend, Jamie. You was prepared to stay with me when the cops was chasing us. I'll never forget it. And if it wasn't for you, we wouldn't have got back.'

Jamie smiled. 'You played your part. You nicked the necklace that got us to see Catherine and you gave Billy a good fight.'

Todd nodded and grinned. 'Yeah, I did, didn't I?'

They reached the playing fields, where someone shouted, 'About time, where've youse been?'

'Don't worry, we're here now,' Todd replied.

'Oi, Jamie!' It was Wayne Carter, the bully. He came bowling across the field, his big frame and bronze highlights fused with his black, unkempt hair, always a formidable sight. 'I've got a good book for you, about space. Me Nan got it me for Christmas, but it's no use to me.'

Jamie smiled. 'Thanks, Wayne.'

'I've got a new catapult, it's French and well wicked, I'll show it to you, later,' Steve called.

'Sounds good.' Jamie felt he had the best of both worlds. He was now friendly with the Riverside Posse, because of his expertise with the catapult, but not affiliated to it. They even let him play football with them now! 'Whose side am I on?'

Wayne Carter piped up. 'We'll have him, seeing as we're winning easily.'

There were titters of amusement as Jamie joined Carter's side.

Jamie looked up at the moon and smiled inside; he was with his new friends *and* his reliable companion.

Now you've read the book, why not follow the Time Trap Trail and get a personalised Time Trap Adventurer's Certificate?

timetrap.co.uk

TEMPLE BAR

Acknowledgements

Pat Richardson, Ken Titmuss, my nephew Carl Smith, Uphall School Ilford, Jean Evans, Professor John Chalker, Sonia Ribeiro, Ian Franklin, my dad George Smith, my brother George Smith, Cornerstones, Hilary Johnson, my sister Sylvia Smith, Brenda Rous and the Fast-Print Publishing team.

And last but not least, my mum, who told me never to give up writing.

All helped through the years to get Time Trap where it is today.